Nathan stood as a young woman entered the room. At first glance he might have mistaken her for a scullery maid.

Her dress was dirty and torn, her aub_____ ___ ___ ___ was tangled, and she was carrying a _____ wers. Yet something in her _____ lark eyes drew his attention_____

"Brother Pierce, I _____ er, Abigail." His hostess r_____ _odding toward the woman who _____ ket on a table that stood inside the door.

He stepped forward with a bow. "It's a pleasure to meet you, Miss LeGrand. Your mother has been saying some nice things about you."

She looked past him with a frown. "I see." She executed a graceful bow in spite of her appearance. "I hope you will make room for a parent's bias as I doubt I can ever measure up to whatever she has told you."

Nathan's mouth dropped open. So much for the demure young woman he'd pictured. While Mrs. LeGrand was the epitome of grace and refinement, it was obvious to him that she had failed to instill the same qualities in her offspring. Even though he had been raised in a far more rustic environment than this young woman, he was surprised by Abigail LeGrand's lack of sophistication. Or was she merely flouting parental control? She was certainly old enough to have a household of her own. The Shakespearean tale of the shrew came to mind. Perhaps all she needed was a strong man to take her in hand as Petruchio had done with his Katherine. He wished the man the best of luck.

DIANE T. ASHLEY, a "town girl" born and raised in Mississippi, has worked more than twenty years for the House of Representatives. She rediscovered a thirst for writing, was led to a class taught by Aaron McCarver, and became a founding member of the Bards of Faith. Visit her at www.bardsoffaith.homestead.com.

AARON McCARVER is a transplanted Mississippian who was raised in the mountains near Dunlap, Tennessee. He loves his jobs of teaching at two Christian colleges and editing for Barbour Publishing. A member of ACFW, he is coauthor with Gilbert Morris of the bestselling series, The Spirit of Appalachia.

Books by Diane T. Ashley and Aaron McCarver

HEARTSONG PRESENTS
HP860—Under the Tulip Poplar
HP879—A Bouquet for Iris
HP892—The Mockingbird's Call
HP920—Across the Cotton Fields

Don't miss out on any of our super romances. Write to us at the following address for information on our newest releases and club information.

Heartsong Presents Readers' Service
PO Box 721
Uhrichsville, OH 44683

Or visit www.heartsongpresents.com

Among the Magnolias

Diane T. Ashley and Aaron McCarver

Heartsong Presents

For my church family at Victory Congregational Methodist Church. Your love and support have always upheld me when I needed it most. I am thankful to be part of such a loving congregation.

Aaron

For John and Pat Bass—You are the inspiration for the characters I named after you. Thanks for the love you have lavished on your nieces and nephews. Sorry that I never quite developed a taste for tuna fish casserole.

Diane

A note from the Authors:
We love to hear from our readers! You may correspond with us by writing:

Diane T. Ashley and Aaron McCarver
Author Relations
PO Box 721
Uhrichsville, OH 44683

ISBN 978-1-61626-244-0

AMONG THE MAGNOLIAS

All scripture quotations are taken from the King James Version of the Bible.

All of the characters and events in this book are fictitious. Any resemblance to actual persons, living or dead, or to actual events is purely coincidental.

Our mission is to publish and distribute inspirational products offering exceptional value and biblical encouragement to the masses.

PRINTED IN THE U.S.A.

prologue

November 1839

"Chattanooga. . ." Nathan Pierce let the syllables roll around in his mouth as he strode down the street toward the tavern at the crossroads. He liked the name of his newly incorporated town. Many others had been suggested, but he felt the Indian word suited the area best. A reminder of the original inhabitants of Tennessee, the people who had been removed to make way for the expansion of the United States. He had done what he could to make their removal easier—giving them food and blankets in an attempt to make their trek easier. But so many had died.

With a heavy sigh, Nathan hunched his shoulders against the cool November air as dusk crept over the town. Drawing even with three women, apparently a mother and her two daughters, he tugged on the brim of his hat. "Good evening."

A chorus of giggles, shushed by the older woman, was the only answer he received from them. They looked vaguely familiar, but Nathan could not recall their names, not an unusual circumstance these days with the flood of settlers coming into the area. Everything was changing. But he couldn't complain too much. Business at Pierce's Dry Goods had become so demanding he had hired two men to help him at the counter, as well as a young boy who swept the floors and dusted the shelves to keep his store gleaming.

Poe's Crossroads was no longer the meeting place for the town council, but it was still a good place to visit to catch up on whatever was happening in the community. And Margaret still performed there nightly. He liked visiting with the lively redhead. She had offered a sympathetic ear back in the days when his heart had been broken by Iris Landon—no, Iris Stuart.

Margaret was playing a lively tune on her piano as he entered the large room. Card games had already started at a couple of tables, and the bar was crowded with eager patrons. He ignored the odor of unwashed bodies and stale beer as he made his way across the room to an empty table near the piano, avoiding wet spots where the sawdust had failed to absorb spills.

Margaret finished playing with a flourish and turned on the piano bench. "You're here early this evening, Nathan."

He nodded. "Charles is going to close up, so I thought I'd come get some supper and see how you're doing."

Her lips turned up. "I'm flattered." She waved at one of the waitresses and held up two fingers before taking a seat at his table. Two cups of coffee were plunked down on the table between them, followed quickly by two plates of meat and potatoes. Margaret folded her hands in her lap and bowed her head, encouraging Nathan to bless the food.

He looked down at his lap. "Lord, thanks for good company and good food. Amen." Raising his head, he picked up his napkin and placed it in his lap. "Let's eat."

It was loud in the room, but they ate in silence. Nathan cleaned every bite of food from his plate and sat back with a contented sigh. "Poe's cook cannot be outdone." He looked toward Margaret's plate and watched as she pushed her food around with her fork. "Is something wrong with your dinner?"

"No," she answered him, shaking her head. "I guess I'm not very hungry."

He stared at her face. Margaret could not be called beautiful in the strictest sense of the word. Her mouth was a little too generous, her nose a tad too long, and freckles covered every inch of her face. But her bright blue eyes and carrot-colored hair made most men look twice. Her personality is what made him seek her out. Margaret was a good friend—undemanding and nonjudgmental. "What's wrong?"

She sighed and put her fork down. "I've been thinking about making a change."

"What kind of change are you talking about?"

Her shoulders lifted in a shrug. "Having more people here makes things complicated."

Nathan frowned. "But you've lived here most of your life."

Everyone knew Margaret's history. Her parents had brought her west on the Tennessee River but perished of disease, leaving her without any knowledge of existing family. Her only connection to her past was the piano she now played for customers here at the crossroads.

"I want to do something more with my life than this." She spread her hands to indicate the tavern. "I'm tired of waiting for something good to happen. I'm ready to make my own future. Do something important with my life."

"Do you have something in mind?"

"Not really. All I know is I'm tired of coming into this place. Tired of being importuned by men who have the wrong idea about me. Tired of being shunned by the women in town."

"They don't know you like I do." He reached out to take her hand in his. "If they did, they'd be proud to call you friend."

Her smile seemed sad to him. Nathan wished he could do something for her. He thought of his bank account. He had enough money to give Margaret a new start no matter where she wanted to go. He opened his mouth to tell her his idea when his chair was bumped. Hard.

He wrinkled his nose as an offensive odor of sweat and grime washed over him. A beefy arm reached across the table and grabbed Margaret's arm, pulling her hand from Nathan's grasp as she was hauled out of her chair. "Whatta' we have here?" His words were slurred, indicating he'd been imbibing freely. "Ye tol' me ye had no time fer bein' friendly. Yet I sees yer holding hands wit' Mr. Fancypants here."

For a split second, Nathan was frozen by shock. How dare someone accost Margaret?

"Let go of me, you oaf." Margaret tried to pull away, but the big man had a tight grip on her arm.

Nathan surged up from his seat. "Let her go." He reached out and grabbed the man's arm, a part of him noticing a puff of dust while the majority of his mind registered the rock-hard muscles of the stranger's biceps.

A rush of energy pumped into his arm, and he swung the stranger around to face him, causing the man to lose his grip on Margaret's arm. Margaret stumbled into the table, knocking it and its contents onto the floor.

"You shoulda' have done that, mister." The drunken man focused his close-set eyes on Nathan. He swung his free hand up and landed a hard blow on Nathan's chin.

Seeing stars for a moment, Nathan lost his grip on the man's arm. He swallowed against the pain and balled his fists. "I don't want a fight."

"Too late." The other man took another swing at him.

This time Nathan saw the move and managed to duck. His opponent stumbled forward, carried by his own weight. Nathan straightened his legs and twisted to follow the other man's movements. He raised his fists to protect his face, knowing there would be no other way out but to defeat the man. Although he would have much preferred a peaceful end to this confrontation, he knew how to fight. His uncle had made certain of that.

As the man turned to continue the attack, Nathan moved forward and landed two heavy jabs—one on his opponent's stomach and another on his chin. The man stumbled back and Nathan followed him, his blood boiling. Another blow to the stomach, followed by a swift uppercut, doubled the man over. Nathan stepped back, panting slightly from his exertion. He glanced around to make certain Margaret was okay, and his foot skidded through a puddle of coffee.

"Look out!" Margaret's cry brought his attention back to the man in time to see the glint of a knife headed in a deadly arc toward his chest.

Time seemed to slow to a crawl. He reached out both hands to stop the hand holding the weapon. It was like trying to stop a wall from falling down on him. His arms shook with the effort. The knife inched closer, slowly taking over his whole field of vision. He was no longer aware of anyone. . .only the honed edge of the blade that now almost tore through his shirt.

Failure loomed, as did the death he had no doubt would swiftly follow the knife's plunge into his chest. In a desperate move, he stepped forward, placing his right leg between the other man's feet, and twisted hard. Caught off guard, the man leaned his upper body forward.

In an instant the situation changed. Nathan felt his opponent's foot slip. The larger man lost his balance and his momentum doomed him. The knife between them resisted briefly before sliding deep into the man's body.

Horrified, Nathan released his tight grip on the man's hand and tried to catch him before he hit the ground. It was a futile effort. The stranger outweighed him by at least two stone. When he hit the floor, he groaned loudly, rolled over. . .and died.

Nathan fell to the floor beside him, uncertain of what to do but wanting to help the man if at all possible. He reached for the knife, whose hilt was protruding from the man's chest, but before he could pull it free, someone grabbed him from behind and lifted him away. Suddenly he was aware of other voices, some frantic, others excited.

Someone came running in and knelt where Nathan had just been. Dr. Robinson. He watched with fading hope as the doctor checked for a pulse, put his ear next to the fallen man's mouth, and finally straightened with a single head shake. "He's dead."

"Good riddance." The voice was Margaret's, but he heard the other men crowded around the body echo the sentiment.

"But I. . .it was an accident." Nathan looked down at his shirt, splattered with blood, and shuddered. He was a murderer. He had taken another man's life. "He slipped and the knife. . ." He felt again the sensation as the knife hesitated then plunged to its hilt, scraping past a bone on its deadly journey. He shuddered, his hands shaking like leaves in a strong wind. "He can't be dead."

Someone patted his shoulder. "It's okay, Nathan. Everyone knows it was self-defense."

"That's right," another man chimed in. "I saw him attack you. It was a fair fight until he pulled out his Arkansas toothpick."

Dr. Robinson stood up and looked at him. "Are you hurt?"

Nathan shook his head.

"Then I'm going back home to my supper." He pointed to the body on the floor. "Only the undertaker can help him now."

The man patting his shoulder spoke again. "God rest his soul."

Nathan turned and pushed his way past the knot of men. The words echoed in his mind. . .*God rest his soul. . .God rest his soul.* He wondered exactly where the slain man's soul was at this instant. Had his untimely death doomed him to eternity in hell? And what would happen to Nathan now? God would surely condemn him for taking another man's life. Why hadn't he found another way out of the situation? Why had he allowed the man's violent nature to rule?

The questions dogged him all the way back to his home. They echoed as he washed away the dead man's blood. They followed him into his bedroom, robbing him of sleep. When he did finally manage to close his eyes, all he could see was the stranger's surprised face, all he could remember was the feel of the knife biting into the other man's flesh. He was as guilty as Cain and deserved whatever punishment God meted out to him.

૨

Christmas was supposed to be a time of love and celebration, but Nathan could find no joy at all. He should not have accepted Iris Stuart's invitation for Christmas dinner.

He glanced around the room at the other guests—Wayha Spencer and his two granddaughters were here. He ought to be glad that they had not lost their home like so many of the other Indians in the area. If not for Iris and Adam's intervention, they would probably not be here.

Lance and Camie Sherer were here, too. They had also brought their children. Just being around such nice families ought to make him feel better—but it didn't.

Adam Stuart walked over to him. "I've got something I need to talk to you about." He inclined his head toward the door. "Let's go to my study for a minute."

Nathan followed him to the quieter room and waited for Adam to speak.

"I'm worried about you, Nathan."

With a sigh, Nathan walked to the window and looked out at the scenery. Last week's snow had mostly disappeared, leaving patches of white here and there in the shadiest parts of the Stuarts' grounds. "Is that why you and Iris invited me?"

"Of course not." Adam's easy chuckle filled the room. "You and I have been friends for years, Nathan. Which is why I feel I need to say something. You haven't been the same since the accident."

"Accident?" Nathan didn't even try to keep the derision out of his voice. "You mean murder. Although it may not have been intentional, I murdered Ira Watson."

Adam walked up behind him and put a hand on Nathan's shoulder. "The Bible speaks to the difference between homicide and accidental death. You know you held no enmity against that man. He attacked you—"

"Not until I stepped between him and Margaret."

"So you are condemning yourself for protecting a lady? A woman who has been your friend for longer than we have? Who could not protect herself from his brute strength?" Adam's hand tightened on his shoulder. "God would not condemn you for protecting the weak."

"How can you speak for God?" Nathan let his anger escape. "How can you say what He thinks? He created Ira Watson and died for his salvation as much as He died for mine."

"That's true, but sadly not all men choose to embrace God. Some refuse to listen until it's too late."

Nathan knew his friend was speaking the truth. He wanted to embrace it, but he could not. "I wish I hadn't gone to eat supper there that night. I wish I'd gone home and eaten alone. I wish someone had stepped in when the fight first broke out. I wish any number of things had happened that night. But they didn't. And—I—killed—Ira Watson."

"If you were guilty, don't you think the sheriff would have arrested you?"

He lifted his shoulders in a shrug. "No one liked the man. He hadn't been here long, so he didn't have anyone to defend him. I couldn't even find any family connections."

"All of that is beside the point. The sheriff is a fair man. When he learned the circumstances surrounding Mr. Watson's death, he knew no reason existed for him to arrest you."

"He's only a man. He should have arrested me. He wasn't inside my head that evening. He didn't know how angry I was. How could he? Only God knows what was in my mind, and I feel the weight of His judgment."

"Listen to me, Nathan." A new tone had come into Adam's voice now. A sound of command. "You have got to find a way to forgive yourself and put that unfortunate episode behind you. Believe me, I know the danger of holding on to the past. I almost waited too long. Every day I thank God for bringing me out of my bitterness. He can heal you, too, if you'll let Him."

Knowing Adam was right, Nathan pinned a smile on his face. "I've been thinking about that."

"I'm glad to hear it." Adam returned his smile. "If there's anything I can do to help, please don't hesitate."

"Just pray for me."

"Always." Adam led the way back to the parlor.

Nathan watched as his friends laughed and talked, wishing he could join in. But an invisible wall seemed to separate them, a wall he didn't know how to break through. Maybe if he had the right tool. . . maybe if he studied his Bible more. . .maybe if he dedicated himself completely to do the Lord's work. . .

The idea took root. He could study more and understand God's Word better if he let go of all his worldly considerations and devoted himself to the Lord's service.

The more he thought of it, the more he liked the idea. He would become a preacher. He'd sell everything he owned—the store and its inventory, his land, his home—everything. He'd go wherever the church sent him. He'd face any hardship with fortitude. And once God saw how devoted he was, maybe He would erase the guilt of Nathan's evil deed.

He said good night to his hosts and assured them he would be better in the days ahead. He watched as a look of relief passed between Iris and Adam. He felt humbled to know he had such good friends. They truly cared about him. He wanted to tell them of the plan he'd come up with after his talk with Adam, but it was too new, too precious. He did not want to risk having anyone put a stumbling block in his way. He knew this was the right thing to do.

Nathan climbed onto his horse and rode home, feeling more hopeful than he'd felt in a month. He glanced up at the clear night sky, thinking of that night more than eighteen hundred years earlier, when God had become man. He was determined to find his way back to the upright man he'd once been.

He would study hard, learn every verse, memorize the whole Bible if he had to. He would show God how penitent he was. He would become worthy again, even if it took him the rest of his life.

one

May 1841

Nathan leaned forward in the saddle. "It won't be long now, Lazarus. We should arrive in Natchez before noon."

The horse nodded as if excited by the promise. Nathan straightened and looked around him. The terrain was so different on the southern section of the Natchez Road. Pine trees crowded in on either side and formed a canopy above horse and rider, offering welcome shade in the warm spring temperatures. Although Nathan was acclimated to warm temperatures—it already felt like summer here in Mississippi even though it was only midmorning—he was already sweating. He supposed many things would be different here.

Should he stay in a hotel in Natchez On-the-Hill before appearing at Magnolia Plantation? He was several days ahead of his scheduled arrival, and he did not want to inconvenience his hosts. Or should he proceed directly to the plantation, which would serve as his home base for the next few years? At least he hoped he would be stationed here for that long before the church decided to give him a new circuit.

He could not wait to see the accommodations being provided by Mr. and Mrs. LeGrand. A separate home for his own use. It would be quite a change from the past year apprenticing under Douglas Feazell. He was looking forward to hours of quiet without the interruption of Pastor Feazell's three rambunctious children.

By all accounts, Mr. and Mrs. Jeremiah LeGrand were a couple with but one child, a young woman with intellectual, rather than family, pursuits. He had no doubt she would be plain, outspoken, or terribly spoiled by doting parents—perhaps all three. But at least she would not pull on his coat to get his attention or try to climb in his lap with sticky fingers.

Nathan's stomach clenched. He did not understand why children were so ill-behaved. He had been a model of propriety from the time he could walk. Everyone said so. Why did other children have to run and romp, scream at nothing, and shout when a whisper was more appropriate?

Nathan took several deep breaths and urged his horse to a canter as the dense foliage began to give way to cultivated fields. He passed an inn and waved to a man sitting on the front porch in a rocking chair. He traveled another mile before seeing a large house in the distance that must be one of the plantation homes. Was it Magnolia Plantation? He had no way of knowing, so he stayed on the road that would take him into town. He would find someone there to give him specific directions.

The bustling port city came into view as he crested a hill. People hurried along wooden boardwalks on errands, and the streets were clogged with wagons, carts, horses, and carriages. The sights and sounds were nearly overwhelming to him. Banks and millinery stores vied for space next to grocers and livery stables. On his left, he caught the shouts and laughter of children running on the lawn of what appeared to be a school or orphanage. He shuddered and moved on as quickly as he could manage.

He allowed his horse to follow other riders moving in a westerly direction and was eventually rewarded by a stunning vista—the wide ribbon of the Mississippi lay at the bottom of a precipice, her muddy waters rushing southward with a flotilla of cargo-laden boats.

Not wanting to actually go down to Natchez Under-the-Hill, he moved out of the flow of foot and horse traffic, choosing a grassy park bordering the main road. The park must have been created for visitors such as him, offering several benches and a hitching post. Nathan dismounted and tethered his horse before walking to one of the benches that overlooked the river below. He breathed deeply of the warm air, removed his hat, leaned back, and closed his eyes to thank God for a safe journey.

A young girl's voice interrupted his prayer. "Hey, mister, are you asleep?"

Nathan opened his eyes to see a girl with hair as blond as his own wearing an oversized dress. She could have been anywhere between the ages of toddler and debutante. "I am not."

The girl pursed her lips and nodded. "Too much to drink?"

He looked around for rescue. The girl must have a nanny or mother somewhere in the vicinity.

"My uncle Freddy used to drink in the morning." She sat down beside him on the bench and swung her feet to and fro. "But then he got mashed by a hotel." The girl smacked one hand down on the other with a loud sound.

"He what?"

She nodded and fixed him with a blue-eyed stare. "A big tormato came here last year and killed lots of people. Uncle Freddy was eating his dinner at the Steamboat and it fell down on him. That's why I had to go to Mercy House and live with the other orphans."

Nathan's mouth dropped open. He ran his hand through his hair, a sure sign of anxiety, and immediately tried to straighten it. "Did you come here alone?"

"Ummm." The girl sneaked a glance past him. "Nooo. But Miss Deborah is busy."

He swiveled his head to see a group of children being gathered up by a tall woman who was frantically looking around. He could understand her concern. His desire to ease her fear overcame his own anxiety. "I think you've been missed."

The girl tried to hide behind his shoulder. "I wanted to see if you were okay."

"Well now that you know I am, why don't you let me return you to your friends?" Nathan stood up and held out a hand to her. He didn't know why he didn't send her on her way, but he could not ignore the sadness in the child's eyes. "Come along. I'll take you back."

"You look like Uncle Freddy. Maybe you could say you're his brother and Miss Deborah would let me come live with you."

"I have many reasons to reject such a suggestion." Nathan tried to keep the horror from his voice. "The first is that it would be a lie. I'm a pastor. Would you have me break one of God's commandments?"

Her eyes widened, and she shook her head.

"Good. Come along, then, Miss. . ."

"Mishal Carpenter, but everyone calls me Mia." She stood up and brushed a leaf from her skirt.

"Miss Carpenter." Feeling a little like he'd been run over by a team of horses, Nathan escorted the precocious child back to her guardian. As he walked away, he could hear the children asking about his identity. He didn't hear what Mia's answer was, but he hoped it had nothing to do with "tormatos" or uncles.

Nathan collected his horse and decided to stop at the land office he'd passed on his way through town. After winding his way through the steady stream of townspeople, he arrived at the glass-fronted building that advertised the business within and the owner, Silas Ward. He dismounted and entered the front door, setting off the tinkling of a bell.

"Hello, what can I do for you?" An olive-complexioned man with dark eyes and darker hair smiled at him from behind a tall counter.

"I need to find out how to get to Magnolia Plantation." Nathan removed his hat and held out a hand to the merchant he imagined to be Mr. Ward. "I'm new to these parts, and I thought you might be able to help me."

The man on the far side of the counter frowned, and his mustache twitched.

Nathan wondered if he had broken some local custom. Back home he could have stopped at any number of businesses to make a similar inquiry, but this was not Tennessee.

"What's your business with the LeGrands?"

Nathan let his hand fall to his side. "I'm the new itinerant pastor, and the LeGrands have graciously offered me a place to stay while I'm holding church meetings here in Natchez."

The man's expression lightened a degree or two. "So you're the new pastor. And here I was thinking you might be a customer."

"Sorry to disappoint you, sir, but I have no need for land." Nathan stretched his mouth in a smile. "I hope that won't keep you from attending church once I am able to take the pulpit."

"Of course it won't." The man extended his hand across the counter. "My name's Silas Ward. Pleased to make your acquaintance, Pastor."

Nathan returned the firm handshake. "Likewise, Mr. Ward." He watched the features on the other man's face, amazed at the transformation. From professional courtesy to distrust to friendliness. Mr. Ward would make a fine actor. But was his ability to modify his temperament at lightning speed an indication of imbalance?

As Mr. Ward described the route he should follow to Magnolia Plantation, Nathan tried to quash his misgivings. It was not his place to judge others. That much he had surely learned in the past year.

He assumed a pleasant smile, thanked the merchant, and escaped with a sigh of relief. His dislike for Mr. Silas Ward was disturbing. He would have to pray for understanding and acceptance. His future as a pastor depended on his ability to relate to all the people in the community.

two

"What's that on your cheek?"

Abigail LeGrand rubbed at her face and sneezed. "Probably dust."

"Let me." Her mother pulled a handkerchief from the pocket of her skirt and stepped close. "You're only making matters worse."

Abigail tapped her foot but submitted to her mother's ministrations. Why wasn't she covered in dust, too? But then no amount of grime would ever take away from her mother's beauty. From the top of her gleaming black tresses to the toes of her fashionable slippers, Mama always looked as though she'd stepped from the covers of a ladies' magazine.

"I don't see why you're so concerned, Mama. We still have a lot to do this afternoon to get the cottage ready for the new minister." She pointed at the pile of dust covers she and her mother had removed from the furniture. "Those need to be washed and stored, and I still have to cut the magnolia blossoms you wanted."

Her mother sighed and looked around. "I always forget what all has to be done, but we need to hurry. The new preacher will be here any day now, and I want everything to be right for him."

"It will be, Mama. You are the perfect hostess, and I'm certain you'll soon have the new pastor eating out of your hand."

"As could you if you would only apply yourself."

"Mother!" Abigail used the tone of voice she reserved for indicating disdain. "I have no desire to endear myself to any man, pastor or not."

"Sometimes I think your papa and I did you a disservice

when we let you talk us into sending you to Elizabeth Female Academy."

Abigail frowned at her. "How can you even think such a thing? Would you have preferred someone like Violeta Sheffield, a simpering debutante with no accomplishments beyond needlework and watercolors?"

"Of course not, but you should not be so patronizing about Lowell and Dorcas's daughter. She is a sweet girl whether she has earned a degree or not."

Her cheeks heated up at the criticism. Abigail knew her mother was right. "I'm sorry, but I get so tired of hearing everyone talk about how accomplished and biddable she is. Does no one in this town appreciate a female who has a little sense?"

Her mother's dark eyes flashed. "You outshine Violeta in every respect. Never doubt that for a moment. But as your mother, I have the right to be concerned about whether or not you will experience firsthand the joy of having a family of your own."

"I spend enough time at the orphanage to give me a good idea of what it's like to provide guidance for children. Besides, you are the one who has always cautioned me to avoid placing all my dependence on a man." Abigail grabbed a cloth and attacked the dust scattered across a rosewood accent table.

Her mother picked up a broom and began sweeping. "I didn't want you to make the mistake of thinking marriage is the only goal a female should have. Your first dependence should always be on God, then on the talents He gave you—"

"Exactly. So why should I want to bury my talents in order to be subservient to some man?" A strand of hair loosed itself from Abigail's tight bun. She pushed it back with one finger as she continued her work. "Besides, most of the men in Natchez would think I'd lost my mind if I tried to talk them into freeing their slaves and adopting the sharecropping methods we use here."

"That's true, dear, and perhaps that is why the Lord is sending us a young pastor." Her mother stopped sweeping and looked into the distance, a tender smile on her face. "A godly man who will see you as the treasure you are."

"I don't understand why you feel it incumbent on me to marry at all. I am perfectly content to live here with you and Papa."

"That's because you don't know how wonderful marriage to the right man can be."

Her mother's words struck a chord in Abigail's heart. She had ample evidence of the joys of a successful marriage, but she didn't think any man as perfect as her father existed. Jeremiah LeGrand was smart, hardworking, thoughtful, and loving—a kind father and a good provider. But most of all, he was a man who put Christ first in his life. She knew her parents had faced hard times because of their beliefs. Even now, some in Natchez chose not to associate with the LeGrand family. But her parents had never seemed to care what others thought. They did as their faith dictated.

"Everything looks very nice." Mama surveyed the gleaming parlor with a smile of approval. "I hope Brother Pierce will be happy here."

"I'm sure he will be, Mama. No one has ever been disappointed here."

"There's always a first time. And this pastor is so much younger than most of the men we have hosted in the past. He might prefer to live closer to town."

Abigail rolled her eyes. "What man in his right mind would prefer the noise and dust of town to all of this?"

"I pray you're right."

"You worry too much." After giving her mother an affectionate hug, Abigail picked up her gardening shears and a shallow basket. "I'll be back in a few minutes with enough magnolia blossoms to freshen every room in the cottage."

"Be careful, dear. Some of those blooms may be too high for you to reach."

"Yes, Mother." Abigail sighed. Would her parents never cease treating her as a child? She was a full-grown woman, a confirmed old maid by most people's estimation. At the ripe old age of twenty-three, Abigail believed she had learned how to rely on herself.

Shaking off her irritation, Abigail concentrated on her self-appointed task. Spring was her favorite time of the year. Dozens of magnolia trees surrounded the grounds, their large, dark green leaves the perfect background for the fragrant white blossoms that had begun to flower in the past weeks. As she moved from tree to tree, selecting the prettiest flowers to scent the pastor's cottage, thoughts of God filled her mind. What a beautiful world He had created. And she was blessed to have the leisure to appreciate it. Why would she ever want to leave Magnolia Plantation? The answer was simple: She wouldn't.

She filled her basket and wandered back across the shade-dappled grounds toward the cottage. It looked exactly like the main house, only smaller. The corners and sides of the cottage were red brick broken by wide windows that let light and cooling breezes into the front parlor. Steps led up to a shady verandah supported by a pair of white columns. The front door was almost wide enough to drive a carriage through and framed by sidelight windows and a transom. Besides the front parlor, the cottage boasted two bedrooms, a dining room, and a small study. Perfect for a single minister or one with a small family.

Abigail climbed the steps and pushed the door open. "I'm back, Mama."

"We're here in the parlor, dearest."

We? Who was in the parlor with her mother? A groan escaped her as she realized the probable identity of the visitor. She put a hand to her hair. Working outside had done nothing for her coiffure. It probably resembled a rat's nest. So much for making a good impression on the new pastor.

Abigail took a deep breath and pinned a welcoming smile on her face. At least her mother wouldn't pester her anymore about trying to make a match with the man.

❧

Nathan stood as a young woman entered the room. At first glance he might have mistaken her for a scullery maid. Her dress was dirty and torn, her auburn-hued hair was tangled, and she was carrying a large basket of white flowers. Yet something in her carriage, some look in her wide, dark eyes drew his attention.

"Brother Pierce, I would like you to meet my daughter, Abigail." His hostess retained her seat on the sofa, nodding toward the woman who was putting her basket on a table that stood inside the door.

He stepped forward with a bow. "It's a pleasure to meet you, Miss LeGrand. Your mother has been saying some nice things about you."

She looked past him with a frown. "I see." She executed a graceful bow in spite of her appearance. "I hope you will make room for a parent's bias as I doubt I can ever measure up to whatever she has told you."

Nathan's mouth dropped open. So much for the demure young woman he'd pictured. While Mrs. LeGrand was the epitome of grace and refinement, it was obvious to him that she had failed to instill the same qualities in her offspring. Even though he had been raised in a far more rustic environment than this young woman, he was surprised by Abigail LeGrand's lack of sophistication. Or was she merely flouting parental control? She was certainly old enough to have a household of her own. The Shakespearean tale of the shrew came to mind. Perhaps all she needed was a strong man to take her in hand as Petruchio had done with his Katherine. He wished the man the best of luck.

"Come sit down, Abigail," her mother admonished her rude daughter. "All I told the pastor was how much we were looking forward to making his acquaintance and that we were ready to do whatever we could to make his stay here more comfortable."

Nathan waited until she did as her mother requested before he returned to his seat in a padded chair next to the fireplace. "Perhaps you ladies would be so kind as to tell me a little about the people in the area I will be expected to reach. Are there many lost souls hereabouts?"

"I'm sure we have our fair share of nonbelievers, Pastor." Mrs. LeGrand answered his query, so he turned his attention to her. "But we also have several ministries in the area that try to reach out to them."

Nathan was eager to get started. The more people he baptized, the more worthy he felt. Perhaps he could eventually wash away the sin he'd once committed. He rubbed his hands together. "I can hardly wait."

Mrs. LeGrand smiled at him. "Perhaps Abigail can introduce you around to some of the townspeople."

A snort from the daughter let him know how she felt about her mother's suggestion. "All you have to do is visit Natchez Under-the-Hill, Brother Pierce. You will find enough lost souls there to keep you busy for quite some time."

Nathan waited for her mother to once again reprimand Abigail, so he was surprised when she nodded.

"Yes indeed." Mrs. LeGrand's words held a note of approval. "Natchez Under-the-Hill is almost a separate town and offers many opportunities for evangelism. We are all involved in a ministry to give aid, hot meals, and blankets to the immigrants and others in need. Perhaps you'd like to join us on Saturday afternoon?"

"It sounds like a wonderful idea, but I suppose I should speak with the church prior to committing my time."

Abigail raised her eyebrows, making Nathan wonder if she ever asked for permission before plunging into a project. He rather doubted it.

Well, part of his duties as a pastor was to provide a good example to the members of the community. He might as well start now by driving home his meaning. "I have an interview with the bishop in Jackson on Wednesday. I should be able to give you a more definitive answer by Thursday."

"Where do you come from, Pastor?" Abigail changed the subject.

"I studied under Pastor Douglas Feazell in Indiana for the past year, but I was born and raised in the southeastern corner of Tennessee. The town's now called Chattanooga."

"I've heard of Chattanooga. And of the poor Indians who were driven away from their homes because gold was discovered nearby. Tell me, Pastor, is it as wild an area as the newspapers report?" Abigail's question had an edge to it. "I have read of gunfights and lawlessness to rival anything that happens in Natchez Under-the-Hill."

Nathan's stomach clenched. Had she heard something of his past? His heart beat so hard he was surprised his shirt was not moving. How could he have dreamed someone so far away would have heard of his crime? He didn't know how to answer the girl. Should he admit his guilt? Or gloss over the past? After all, the people who were there that day had proclaimed him innocent of murder. The silence in the room lengthened as his mind bounced back and forth like an out-of-control stagecoach.

Mrs. LeGrand must have realized how uncomfortable he was. She stood up and straightened her skirts. "Why don't we leave Mr. Pierce alone, Abigail. I'm sure he'd like some time to wash off the dust of the road and settle into his new home."

Abigail hesitated a moment before nodding her agreement.

Mrs. LeGrand walked toward the door but turned back to him before she exited. "I'll ask John to bring you some hot water for a nice bath. He's Mr. LeGrand's personal gentleman, and he'll know exactly what to do to make you more comfortable."

"That's not necessary." He didn't want to be a burden to the LeGrands. "I haven't been waited on in a long time."

She smiled at him. "Then I have no doubt you will enjoy his help. Oh, and don't worry about being late for dinner. We never sit down before eight o'clock to give my husband time to wash after he returns from the fields."

"Dinner?" Nathan shook his head. "I'd not thought to dine with you—"

"You might as well acquiesce gracefully, Brother Pierce." When Abigail smiled, he could see the family resemblance. "I assure you my mother will not take no for an answer."

Nathan sighed as he followed the ladies to the front door. He had the feeling life here at Magnolia Plantation would not be without its challenges. He only hoped he could navigate his way through the choppy waters of the LeGrand family relationships. As an only child, he didn't have a lot of experience in such matters. Perhaps he would be best served to avoid the members of the family altogether.

With a nod he made his decision. He would spend most of his time at other communities in his circuit. After dinner tonight, the LeGrands would hardly ever see him.

three

"I wish my hair was as thick as Mama's. It would make it so much easier to style." Abigail looked at Jemma's reflection in the mirror. Jemma had been part of the LeGrand household since Abigail's parents got married. Even though she could have left early on, when they gave her her freedom, she had opted to remain here and work as a lady's maid. Although the housekeeper was supposed to be the manager of the household staff, everyone turned to Jemma to solve household problems.

Jemma had dressed her mother's hair for as long as Abigail could remember, and she also helped Abigail on special occasions. Not that this was a special occasion. It was only dinner, after all. The same meal she took with her parents every evening. The only difference would be the presence of the new pastor.

"It's not like you to envy others, Abby." The pet name Jemma had given her since she was born gave her a feeling of familiarity and calmed her nervousness. "But never fear. Your hair looks quite nice. See how it gleams in the light of the candles. Everyone at dinner will notice."

Abigail caught the look in the family servant's gaze and blushed. She was grateful Jemma didn't comment on how out of character it was for her to request help to dress for a family dinner.

She cleared her throat and turned her head this way and that to marvel at the hairstyle. Jemma had swept her hair back and up, forming intricate swirls and weaving into them a strand of emerald beads to match Abigail's dress. "You are a genius, Jemma." She stood up and hugged her. "I don't think anyone else could do as good a job as you."

"Go on with you." The maid returned her hug and stepped back. "Let me help you with your dress."

"No thank you." Abigail waved her away. "I appreciate your offer, but I'll be fine."

After Jemma left, Abigail walked over to the bed and stared at the green dress lying across it. She'd had a hard time striking the perfect balance between an informal family dinner and a dinner party with guests. The last time she wore this particular dress, her dinner partner had remarked on the way it enhanced the color of her eyes.

She wandered back to the mirror to stare at her face. Reddish brown hair, brown eyes. She wrinkled her nose and stuck out her tongue at the dull reflection. She looked like a washed-out copy of her mother. Expelling a sigh, she clipped a pair of emerald earrings to her earlobes and removed her wrapper. Then Abigail returned to the bed and slipped her dress over her head. After twisting this way and that, she managed to fasten most of the buttons. Perhaps she should not have sent Jemma out so quickly, but it was too late to call her back now.

The casement clock in the hall chimed the quarter hour, reminding Abigail of the time. She tugged at the full sleeves to bring them down to her wrists and tied them quickly, hoping they were secure enough to stay out of her soup bowl. Something about her dress felt odd, but she didn't have time to check for problems. Instead she searched in her bureau for a shawl which she draped over her shoulders to hide any imperfections and made her way to the dining room.

As she reached the doorway, she heard her father's deep voice welcoming the new pastor. She hesitated a moment in the hall and put a hand to her chest. Why was her heart beating so? "It's only a family dinner," she whispered to herself. "No reason to be nervous. He's a man like any other. His opinion means nothing to you." After a few deep breaths, she pinned a smile to her lips and stepped inside the room.

Her father turned and opened his arms. "Good evening, daughter."

Abigail walked into his embrace. "Hi, Papa. How has your day been?"

"Excellent. I trust yours was as well." He stepped back and looked down at her. "Are you cold? I see you are wearing a shawl. Do you think I should light a fire?"

"Oh no, Papa. It was a bit cool in my bedroom and I thought I'd better bring my shawl to ward off any drafts."

"If you're sure."

Abigail wished she was not the center of attention. "Tell me about your day, Papa."

He shrugged. "I was telling Brother Pierce here about my idea for cultivating a new strain of peas."

Abigail turned to him. "I didn't realize you were a farmer."

His look turned sheepish. "I'm not, but I have some friends who are well versed in planting and harvesting crops."

"I see." She glanced upward and wondered how tall Nathan Pierce was. He easily topped her father, who was nearly six feet tall. She wondered why such a handsome man had not married. Was he so devoted to God that he'd not found time to court? Or had his heart been broken in the past by some coldhearted debutante, causing him to avoid romantic entanglements?

"What did you do prior to answering the Lord's call to the ministry?" her father asked.

"I owned a dry goods store back home."

Abigail's mother walked in. "I apologize for my tardiness."

"Don't worry about it, my dear." Abigail's father left her standing next to Nathan and kissed her mother on the cheek. "You are always worth waiting for."

"And you are ever the gentleman, dearest." She turned her attention to their guest. "I am so glad you were able to join us, Brother Pierce. We would have been devastated if you had not, wouldn't we, Abigail?"

Abigail looked up at the pastor. His cheeks had darkened at her mother's words. How she longed to say something that would ease his discomfort. But nothing came to mind, so she simply nodded.

"Since we are all arrived, why don't we take our places?" Abigail's mother put her hand on her husband's arm and allowed him to lead her to her seat at the foot of the table.

Nathan bowed to Abigail and held out his arm. "Miss LeGrand?"

She put her hand on his arm. The contact, even through the material of his coat, made her fingers tremble.

"You *are* cold." He placed his hand over hers.

Abigail could feel her mother's concerned gaze. "I'm fine." The words were for both of them.

Nathan led her to a chair and pulled it out for her.

She sat down with a sigh of relief. How foolish to have worn the heavy woolen shawl. She could even feel a prickle of heat where it covered her back. Feeling trapped, she squirmed in the chair and tried to ease the shawl away from her arms so she could cool off a little.

He sat opposite her and spoke easily to both her parents. Abigail offered little to the conversation, but she enjoyed watching the expressions cross the new pastor's face. He was not as rustic as one might have thought for a man raised in an untamed corner of Tennessee. She learned that he'd sold all his worldly goods before leaving to work under an itinerant pastor for a year. She admired his ability to walk away from all that was familiar to him and put his faith in God. Abigail wished she had that much courage.

"Don't you agree, Abigail?" Papa's voice garnered her attention.

What was the question? She glanced from one of the faces to the other. "I. . .uh. . .yes, I agree."

From the shocked look on her mother's face, her answer was wrong. Papa coughed and hid his mouth behind his napkin for a moment, apparently laughing at her. When he put it back down in his lap, his expression was matter of fact. "Well, since that's settled, we'll see you the first thing in the morning, Nathan. I know you and Abigail will have a good time on your outing."

Her mother pushed back her chair. "Why don't we retire to the parlor, Abigail, and leave the men to join us in a few minutes."

Abigail nodded and pushed back her own chair, relieved the meal was over but concerned about what she had gotten herself into by not attending the conversation more closely. The material of her dress tautened at the waist, squeezing her stomach as she rose from the table. Then she felt a pop and the material loosened. With a gasp, she grabbed her shawl and pulled it back up to her shoulders. Would the evening never end?

"I am pleased you agreed to take Nathan to town tomorrow. He'll probably want to visit his new church, and I'm sure he'll be interested in seeing the orphanage. He has such a good heart. I know he'll want to work with them like Pastor Ogden used to do." Her mother took her usual place on the horsehair sofa and patted the space next to her. "Is something wrong, dear? You didn't seem your usual self at dinner. Are you feeling poorly?" She laid her hand on Abigail's forehead. "You're burning up!"

Abigail stopped her mother from raising an alarm by grabbing her hand. "I'm fine. I just had a little trouble getting dressed."

Her mother sat back against the sofa. "I thought Jemma helped you. I know she did your hair."

"Yes, but I was so. . .so wrapped up in daydreams that I sent her away too soon." Abigail bit her lip. She'd almost admitted her distraction. Where was her mind tonight? She needed to pull herself together. "I. . .I must not have gotten the back buttoned up properly."

Her mother choked back a laugh. "So that's why you are wearing your winter shawl."

Abigail's face flushed. "Yes, ma'am. I feel like such an idiot, but I couldn't explain."

"I can see you were in a quandary." Mama's eyes danced, increasing Abigail's misery. "Let me see if I can fix it before the men come in."

"I can't."

"Why not?"

"When I got up from the table, I'm pretty sure one of the buttons broke off and rolled under the table. I only hope Na—Brother Pierce—doesn't find it."

This time her mother could not control her laughter. She giggled, snorted, and hooted.

At first Abigail wanted to be offended, but then the humor of the situation got through to her. She joined her mother, and soon they were holding onto each other, tears streaming down their faces.

☙

Nathan wondered what could possibly be so hilarious to Mrs. LeGrand and her daughter. Had they been laughing at him? He shrugged off the thought. They surely had more interesting topics of conversation than the habits of a newcomer.

"What are the two of you laughing about?" His host asked the question he would have liked to ask.

"It's nothing." Mrs. LeGrand took out a handkerchief and dried her eyes. "Only a discussion about la—ladies' fashions." A giggle threatened to choke her words. "I'm sure it would bore you men."

Nathan followed Mrs. LeGrand's gaze to Abigail's face, which had turned bright red. He felt like an interloper within this intimate family gathering. The closeness of the

LeGrand family set off a feeling of loneliness inside him. He had no idea why.

Wait. Hadn't he decided to devote his time and energy to the Lord? Wasn't it essential for him to do so because of his past actions? His future did not include a family, so he'd better get his mind focused on what really mattered.

A silver service dominated the table in front of the sofa, and the rich aroma of fresh coffee filled the air. He took one of the two chairs facing the sofa on the far side of the table while Mr. LeGrand seated himself in the other. Mrs. LeGrand poured a cup of the dark brew and handed it to him. He waited to sample the coffee until she had finished serving everyone.

Mr. LeGrand swallowed a mouthful of his coffee and sat back with a sigh. "Excellent, Alexandra."

"Thank you, dear." She turned her dark gaze on Nathan. "Why don't you tell us what things are like in Chattanooga. I know it must have been awful to witness the trials of the Cherokee."

"Yes." His cup rattled as he put it back in its saucer. "The loss of life was most unfortunate."

Abigail's eyes opened wide. "Unfortunate?"

He could feel his cheeks burning. Apparently he had not been forceful enough in his description. While he had never condoned the removal, he had understood President Jackson's reason for doing so.

Mr. LeGrand cleared his throat and shook his head at Abigail as soon as she looked in his direction. "Yes, it was terrible. Forcing people to leave their homes is a harsh solution."

Mrs. LeGrand nodded her agreement before turning to him. "Do you keep in touch with your relatives, Brother Pierce?"

"I'm afraid I have no relatives left. My parents died when I was a young boy. I was raised by my aunt and uncle and inherited their store after they passed away." Although he was grateful for the change of subject, Nathan didn't want to go into any detail about Uncle Richard's demise. His death in prison after the conviction of kidnapping was not something the LeGrands needed to know. "Why don't you tell me more about Magnolia Plantation? Has it been in your family for generations?"

Mr. LeGrand laughed. "Actually I purchased Magnolia about twenty-five years ago, after I arrived in Natchez."

"Is that right? I cannot imagine anyone wanting to leave such a beautiful home."

"It's a long story, but the short version is that Judah Hughes and I came to a mutually beneficial agreement. You'll meet him before long. He and his wife, Susannah, manage a very successful shipping business in town."

"My husband is being modest, as usual." Mrs. LeGrand tossed a fond look at her spouse. "He brought Magnolia Plantation back from the edge of ruin after Judah was wounded in the Battle of New Orleans. If not for him, Judah might not have made it back to Natchez. When they did arrive, my husband rolled up his sleeves and joined the slaves out in the fields."

"In the Lord's eyes, I'm no better than any other man."

"Papa set all of our slaves free as soon as he bought the plantation." Abigail's face showed her pride.

"That's interesting." Nathan's brows furrowed. "I thought all the planters here depended on slave labor to harvest their crops."

"Yes, but I felt setting the slaves free and paying them for their services was a better and more humane way to run this plantation," Mr. LeGrand said. "And you can see for yourself that we have a comfortable lifestyle."

"You supply the land?"

Mr. LeGrand nodded. "And comfortable housing, as well as some of the seed."

"Jeremiah is careful to make sure all of our tenants have everything they need, and then he takes a very small percentage of the proceeds from them," Mrs. LeGrand added.

"What do your neighbors think of your system?"

Abigail leaned forward and put her cup and saucer on the table. "They don't much like it, but it's hard to argue with success. Everyone in Natchez knows about our sharecroppers. They'd like nothing better than for Magnolia Plantation to fail, but every year we do better than before."

"The Lord has blessed us." Mrs. LeGrand dropped a lump of sugar into her coffee and stirred. "So how can we hold a grudge against those who do not agree with us?"

Nathan sensed the LeGrands were not telling the whole story. Slavery was an issue many people felt strongly about. This family had probably had to endure snubs and slurs for their stance, if not worse. They were to be admired.

He wondered if that was why Abigail was unmarried. She certainly had a keen mind. He found himself watching her as she spoke to her parents. Except for a tendency to fidget, she seemed an excellent choice for some lucky suitor. And she would obviously inherit this beautiful estate. She probably had a multitude of young men pursuing her and her family's wealth. Perhaps she even enjoyed their attention and encouraged them to vie against each other. He ran a finger under the collar of his shirt and wondered why the idea of her flirting with a string of hopeful beaus made him feel uncomfortable.

He shook off the feeling and smiled at Mr. and Mrs. LeGrand. "This has been a pleasant evening, but I believe it's time for me to return to my new home. Thank you for inviting me for dinner." He pushed himself up with an effort. The long wearisome trip had apparently caught up with him. Every muscle in his body ached, and he felt like he was at least one hundred years old.

"We are so excited to have you here." Mrs. LeGrand's

eyes sparkled in the candlelight. "I hope you will join us for meals whenever you are here. Even though the cottage has a kitchen, you'll probably find it easier to simply show up here. There's always plenty to go around."

Mr. LeGrand stood up. "Yes, there is." He patted his flat stomach. "And I need help to keep from getting so heavy I can't work out in the fields."

Nathan laughed. "I'm sure you can outwork me any day of the week."

"Get a good night's sleep, Pastor." Abigail folded her hands in her lap. "We can leave right after breakfast."

He bowed to her and her mother. "Thank you for your warm welcome, ladies. I never dreamed I would enjoy such luxury as all of this. And thank you, especially, Miss LeGrand, for making time for me tomorrow. Good night."

Nathan left the plantation home and walked across the manicured lawn to his new home, enjoying the serenade of the crickets. What a peaceful place this was. He glanced up at the twinkling stars in the velvety sky above. "Thank You, God."

Weariness settled on his shoulders as he opened the front door and lit a lamp with the tinder box he found on the mantel. He made his way to a bedroom, stripped off his clothing, and fell into the feathery softness of his bed. His eyes were nearly shut by the time his head settled on the pillow, and as Nathan drifted into slumber, he thought life as an itinerant pastor was far easier than he'd ever dreamed it could be.

four

Birdsong awoke Abigail the next morning. She stretched her arms above her head and yawned. A feeling of euphoria filled her for no apparent reason. Why did she feel so. . .expectant? As though something wonderful was about to happen. Was it the birds outside her window? Although her mother had often told her night air was bad for her constitution, Abigail often raised her window after everyone else had retired. She breathed deeply of the early morning air that was cool with a bare hint of the warmth that would come later.

She did love springtime. She enjoyed watching the bees buzz from one bloom to another before using their tiny wings to lift their cumbersome, fuzzy bodies into the air. As a young girl, she had often followed the bees across the plantation grounds and into the woods, amazed to watch them enter a hive and deposit their load of nectar before heading out once more on their never-ending search.

Rolling over to prop herself on her elbows, Abigail breathed a prayer of appreciation for the natural beauty God had created. The large oak tree outside her window seemed to have leafed out overnight. It never ceased to amaze her how everything seemed to turn green at once. Movement drew her attention, and she watched a pair of gray squirrels chase each other around the upper trunk of the tree. They disappeared after a moment or two, and her gaze traveled farther across the lawn to the roof of the guest cottage.

Brother Pierce. . .Nathan. Her breath caught. Her heart skipped a beat. She was supposed to take him to town this morning and show him the sights. She jumped out of bed with a renewed sense of energy. Not that she was looking forward to seeing him. She was excited to be able to share the town she loved with someone new, someone who didn't yet know all the nooks and crannies of her home.

As she dressed in her riding habit, this time waiting for Jemma's help to get her buttons properly fastened, Abigail wondered where they should start. Should she introduce him to the waterfront missionaries? As a minister, she felt sure he would want to be involved with those who offered food, blankets, and the Word of God to the immigrants and dockworkers. Or maybe she should take him by the church where he would soon be preaching.

Walking into the dining room, she found her mother still breaking her fast. "Has Papa already gone outside?"

Her mother put down her cup and nodded. "You just missed him."

Abigail bent to kiss her mother's cheek. "I admit I spent some time admiring nature from my bedroom window instead of getting dressed and coming downstairs right away."

"You look very nice this morning." Mama picked up a piece of toast and lavished it with blackberry jelly as Abigail moved to her chair. "But why are you wearing your riding habit? I thought you would take the pastor to town in the buggy so you could tell him all about Natchez during the ride."

She shook her head. "I'd rather gallop across the fields on a day like today. It's too pretty to be confined to the roadways."

"And that's why you are still single, my dear." Her mother handed Abigail a plate of scrambled eggs. "You cannot engage a gentleman's attention unless you are close enough to converse with him. Besides, I get the feeling our new pastor is quite refined. He reminds me of the young men I used to know in New Orleans. He would probably rather not be on horseback since he is going to have such a beautiful companion."

Abigail rolled her eyes. "Only you would call me beautiful,

Mama. Some might have considered me attractive when I was younger, but I am far too old for any man to be interested in courting me."

"I'll admit you're not a simpering debutante, but you have many admirable qualities." Mama frowned at her. "And at twenty-three years of age, I don't think you are quite at your last prayers."

"I will be twenty-four next month, and then next year I will be a quarter of a century old." Abigail unfolded the linen napkin next to her plate and placed it in her lap. "Far too old for marriage and children. Not that I am complaining. I am very content with my work at the orphanage in town. God has given me so many opportunities to care for those in need. He knows I do not need a man to be happy with my life."

The words came easily to Abigail. She had said them many times before. And they were true. She leaned on the Lord's strength and had no desire to submit to the will of a husband.

The frown on her mother's face deepened. "Sometimes I think your father and I raised you wrong. We wanted to make sure you had the freedom to wait for the right man to marry, but we may have made you too independent." She reached across the table.

Abigail put down her fork and placed her hand in her mother's. "How can you say such things, Mama? Are you so unhappy with my living here?"

"Not at all." Her mother's grip tightened around Abigail's hand. "But I want you to experience the joys of marriage and motherhood."

Surprised to see a sheen of tears in her mother's eyes, Abigail pulled her hand away and stood up. She rushed to the other side of the table and put her arms around her mother's shoulders. "Do not worry so, Mama. I love you very much, and I'm grateful for the upbringing you and Papa gave me. Perhaps one of these days God will send a special man I can marry, but isn't it better to wait on His provision than to rush into marriage with the wrong spouse?"

"Of course you are right." Her mother put her arms around Abigail's waist and squeezed her tightly. "I want you to have as fulfilling a marriage as your father and I have."

"I don't know how I could be any happier than I am living here with you and Papa." Abigail stood next to her mother for several minutes before moving back to her side of the table. "But if the right man comes along, don't worry. I'll snap him up faster than a hungry alligator could."

Mama's face relaxed as she laughed at Abigail's words. "I do believe you would."

They went on to talk about plans for the day. Soon her mother excused herself and left Abigail to finish her breakfast. She considered her mother's suggestion to take a carriage to town but rejected it. The day was far too glorious. Besides, she wasn't interested in making a match with the new pastor.

Would there ever be a man she would feel comfortable enough with to marry? Abigail didn't know, but she did know one thing—Pastor Nathan Pierce might be attractive, but he was not the man for her. She would never marry an itinerant pastor. The thought of being separated from her home and family was too unbearable.

≈

Nathan felt he had entered a foreign country. Never in his life had he heard so many dialects being spoken. It reminded him of the story in Genesis. Was this what Babel had sounded like when God confounded the speech of the tower builders?

"And this is our new pastor, Nathan Pierce." Miss LeGrand glanced in his direction after introducing him to the ladies working in the soup line.

What was he supposed to say to them? He let his glance move from one expectant face to another. Black and white, young and old, they were waiting to hear what he had to say. "I commend you for your work here."

Smiles answered his first statement. Buoyed by their approval, Nathan breathed more easily. "In the Good Book, the Lamb of God gave us instructions to clothe and feed those in need. You are following His guidance, and I know He is smiling down on all of you. When the time of winnowing comes, you can be confident you will receive His thanks and the richest rewards of heaven."

Miss LeGrand touched his elbow. "We should let them get back to work."

"Yes, of course." He glanced down at her face and wondered if she approved of his words to the ladies. Then he wondered why he cared. He followed her through the rows of cots on which the immigrants sat or lay and watched as she greeted them with warmth and concern. She must come often judging by the way these people responded to her questions about their health and families.

Nathan was impressed by the waterfront facility. He hadn't known what to expect, but after walking through the mean streets of Natchez Under-the-Hill, he had been pleasantly surprised by the large building that was used as dining room by day and dormitory at night. Several windows in the square room allowed natural sunlight in and provided a commanding view of the busy waterfront outside. In a far corner of the room, he could see a man talking to a group of young people. "Who is that?"

Abigail looked in that direction. "That is my uncle John. His wife is my grandmother's sister. They are the ones who started the mission." She walked toward the older gentleman as she explained.

Uncle John stood up and hugged her before turning his gaze on Nathan. "Are you our new preacher?" He held out his right hand.

"Nathan Pierce, at your service, sir." Nathan immediately

liked the man whose hand he was shaking. Tall, with a head full of snowy white hair, he was the type of man one knew immediately could be counted on.

"John Bass." The older man's blue eyes twinkled. "My wife and I are eager to hear your sermons, Pastor."

"I pray they will meet your expectations, sir."

Mr. Bass nodded. "I'm sure they will. What brings the two of you down to the waterfront today?"

"Papa wanted me to show the pastor around town," said Abigail. "But we need to get going, Uncle John. We have several other stops to make."

"It was a pleasure to meet you, Mr. Bass."

"I'm sure we'll see each other often, Pastor. We welcome your guidance as we try to do our Christian duty."

As they left the mission, Nathan wondered if he would be able to offer the guidance Abigail's uncle spoke of. Suddenly he felt unworthy of the position he'd been given. He didn't know enough to lead others. What had he been thinking? Panic seized his throat, and fear nearly brought him to his knees. He stumbled a bit before catching himself.

You have no other choice. Not if you want to wash away your sins. Not if you want to earn God's forgiveness. And what other option is there? Do you want to burn in hell for your misdeeds? Of course not. So you will go forward.

He felt slightly better after giving himself the mental lecture. He was a grown man, and he had studied under one of the best itinerant pastors. He was ready. He had to be ready. Taking a deep breath and shading his eyes from the bright sunlight, he followed Abigail back through the warren of streets.

A man lay facedown in the middle of the road ahead of them, and Nathan reached out a hand to capture Abigail's elbow. He might not be certain of his ability to shepherd others, but he did know how to handle this situation. "Please stand behind me while I check on him."

He could see the surprise in her glance, but she did not pull away from him. "You should not bother the man. He's probably sleeping off a night of excessive alcohol consumption."

Nathan ignored her advice as he bent over the unconscious man. A snore from the prostrate form proved Abigail's advice was sound. He flipped the man over with careful hands. "I don't want someone to run over him."

"Not likely. Not here. There's probably a drunk asleep on nearly every corner of Natchez Under-the-Hill. The saloons fill them with cheap alcohol before robbing them of their money and kicking them out to make room for the next target."

He dragged the man out of the street and into the shade of the livery stable. "Maybe he'll be safe here until he wakes." He reached inside his pants pocket and withdrew the pouch that held his money. It was much slenderer than when he'd started his journey, but he still had enough to help this poor fellow. He withdrew a couple of coins and stuck them inside the pocket of the man's waistcoat. "Maybe you can afford better accommodations with this."

When he straightened it was to find her looking at him with a quizzical expression in her intelligent dark eyes. Nathan wondered if he had broken some local taboo. But hadn't she brought him down here to show him the mission work being done on the riverfront? Or did her sympathy only lie with those who sought shelter in the facility behind them?

"I admire your kindness, Pastor. Your instincts may need some work, but the desire to help others is the first mark of a worthy minister." She waited until he reached her side before moving on.

All morning she had been leading the way, but now she allowed him to tuck her hand under his elbow. Nathan felt taller as she looked up at him. Had he finally won her approval? Ever since meeting Miss Abigail LeGrand, he had felt he was being carefully measured and tested. Her current approving attitude was a distinct change and one he welcomed. He would need all the support he could muster to succeed. "What all do your aunt and uncle do at the mission?"

She nodded to the riverbank where a hodgepodge of boats, from multi-storied steamboats to flat-bottom keelboats and narrow dugout canoes, vied for space. "Those boats bring immigrants streaming into the area. People who have nothing but the clothes they are wearing. They get here so hungry and frightened, so unsure of what the future holds. All we do is offer them a hot meal, a couple of blankets, and a safe place to spend the night."

"That sounds like a lot to me." Nathan compared this waterfront to his home in Tennessee. The people who had been traveling on those boats generally had possessions. Except for the Indians who had been removed from their homelands. "We had a similar group back in Chattanooga. They gave food and blankets to the Indians who were being moved out West."

He saw Abigail's shoulders rise and heard her sigh. "What a sad time for them."

"Yes, but I find myself agreeing with the actual relocation."

She pulled away from him. "How can you say such a thing?"

Now he sighed. "I don't know what it's been like for the Indians and the white people in this part of the country, but where I'm from, there has always been a great deal of friction. Friction that caused pain and death on both sides. There was simply not enough room for both peoples to coexist. I cannot say I agree with the forced march that killed so many of the Indians—"

"How progressive of you."

He ignored her interruption. Miss LeGrand was very outspoken, but she seemed to be very intelligent. Perhaps if he explained the real situation she would understand. "But I do think President Jackson was right giving them their own land west of the river."

Abigail faced him, her fists resting on her hips. "And I suppose you also think it is a good idea to enslave Africans and force them to work their whole lives to provide luxuries for planters."

"Of course not."

"That's a relief."

Nathan ran a finger between his collar and his throat. "No one could condone tearing innocent people from their homes and families and bringing them across the world to work for uncaring landowners."

"Do I hear a hesitation in your voice?"

He cleared his throat and nodded. "Once they have been brought here, without money or training, how can they be expected to stand on their own feet and make a living for themselves? They need kind, considerate landowners to provide for them." He could see her eyebrows drawing together. "In exchange, they provide the labor the landowners need to produce crops. As long as they aren't abused, I don't see anything particularly wrong with the system."

Abigail's mouth dropped open. Her eyes had grown as large as saucers. "You don't see anything wrong with one human being *owning* another?"

He shook his head. "I take it you disagree with my opinion."

"Brother Pierce, that is a gross understatement." She marched off in a huff, leaving him standing alone on the sidewalk.

Passersby looked at him curiously, but no one stopped. Nathan wondered whether he should catch up with her and apologize for expressing his honest opinion. But she had asked, after all. He took a deep breath and followed her. If she could not abide an opposing viewpoint, perhaps she was not as intelligent as she first appeared.

five

Abigail could not wait to tell her mama their new pastor's position on slavery. How could he even call himself a pastor? How could he read the Bible, see the love that Jesus held for His fellow men, and look favorably on the enslavement of human beings? So deep was her disgust that she marched all the way up the hill to Natchez On-the-Hill without slowing.

When she reached the hitching post where they'd tethered their horses, she finally thought to look back to see if he had followed her. She was almost disappointed to see his tall figure marching toward her, his blond hair blown by a fresh breeze from the river's currents. She would have liked to abandon him here, but she supposed she would have to wait.

"Abigail!" A voice drew her attention back to the park. She recognized the Thorntons' carriage and Charlotte's brown curls bobbing as she waved enthusiastically. "Abigail!"

"Hi, Charlotte." She did not have to force the smile raising her lips as the carriage drew near. "Where are Eli and Sarah?"

"I left them at the shop with my parents. Mama insisted, although I'm not sure Papa was as pleased."

"If I know Uncle Judah, he is as happy as a new puppy. He's probably showing little Eli all the secrets of the shipping business."

Charlotte giggled. "You're right. But since Mama is most likely spoiling my daughter with cookies and fresh-baked cake, it only seems fair."

Both of them laughed. Having grown up spending nearly as much time in the Hugheses' home as she had at Magnolia Plantation, Abigail knew her friend was right. "I may have to go and visit your mother."

"She would love to see you. She was saying the other day that you do not come by as often as you used to."

"I know, but my children take so much of my time." Abigail stopped speaking as she felt a presence behind her. She turned around and looked up into the pastor's face. The pastor's shocked face. "I didn't mean—"

"Who is your companion?" Charlotte's query interrupted her explanation.

Reminded of her manners, Abigail decided to drop the matter. Let the silly man believe what he wanted. She performed the introductions and stood silently while Charlotte and the pastor spoke briefly.

"I suppose I'd better get back to my shopping." Charlotte smiled at both of them. "It's a pleasure to welcome you to Natchez. You are in very good hands. Abigail knows everyone."

Brother Pierce bowed and nodded his head. "I'm sure you are right."

Abigail wondered why she didn't believe him. She glanced toward the carriage, surprised to see the lack of understanding in her friend's expression. How could Charlotte miss the irony in his voice? She unhitched her horse and walked toward a nearby mounting block. She swung herself up and looked back at him. "Shall we continue?"

"Am I keeping you from other duties, Miss LeGrand?"

Her cheeks burned. She lifted her chin. "My children? Not at all. I'm about to take you to meet them."

He swung onto his horse and turned its head toward her mount. "I really don't—"

She touched her heels to the horse's flanks and cantered off. Judgmental boor. How dare he take that condescending tone with her?

She fumed as they traveled through the bustling streets of town. Several people hailed her, but she waved at them without slowing down. She was much too irritated to make polite conversation. Besides, she could hardly wait to see what the arrogant pastor would think when he saw her children. Stopping in front of a two-story home that was separated from the traffic by a whitewashed fence, she dismounted and tied her horse to a ring in one of a pair of cast-iron hitching posts shaped like the heads of eagles.

"Miss Abigail." A chorus of voices greeted her entrance into the yard. In only a few seconds, she was surrounded by a group of eager children.

She laughed at them and pulled pieces of hard candy from her reticule. She never came here without treats for them. Her ire melted away as she watched their faces. These children were so thrilled by small things.

"So these are your children?" His voice was not as cold as it had been when they left the park. "I thought—"

"You don't have to tell me what you thought." She frowned at him and indicated the youngsters who still encircled her. "I could hear it in your voice."

One of the younger boys tugged on her skirt. "We have company, Miss Abigail."

She ruffled the boy's hair, aware that he thought himself too old for hugs or kisses. "This is Pastor Nathan Pierce, Joseph."

"No." He looked solemnly at the tall man beside her. "We have more company."

She could hear a choked sound behind her. Was Brother Pierce laughing at Joseph? If he had seen the frightened little tyke when he was first delivered here by one of the boat captains he would not laugh so hard. Joseph's parents died on the journey upriver. Abigail turned around to give the man a piece of her mind and found that he was not even paying any attention to her conversation with Joseph.

He had acquired an admirer. Mia Carpenter had wrapped her arms around one of his legs and was holding on with all her might. "Did you come to get me?"

"No." The man looked like he thought he was about to be

skinned. His cheeks had flushed, and he was trying to pry the child's hands away from his pants. "I came with Miss Abigail."

Abigail felt Mia's questioning glance and nodded. "We need to go inside, dear. Let go of him."

Although the young girl's lower lip trembled, she complied. Satisfied, Abigail turned and led the way onto the shaded porch. A breeze lifted the corners of her hat, and she raised one hand to hold it secure while she opened the front door.

"Deborah, it's Abigail and the new pastor," she called out to the woman who was the matron of the orphanage as she stepped into the entry hall. The parlor was the first door to the left, but she waited for Brother Pierce to join her before entering.

His shoulders filled the doorway, and for a moment Abigail forgot her aggravation. Who would have thought a preacher could be so. . .handsome? The word popped into her head unbidden.

"Hello there."

Abigail told herself the thumping of her heart was because Deborah had surprised her. It had nothing to do with the pastor. He was a man. No different from dozens she had met in the past. And no different from dozens more she would meet in the future. She shook off the thoughts and turned to her friend.

A wide smile and sparkling brown gaze belied the austerity of Deborah's coiffure. Pulled back tightly from her face and twisted into a bun at the base of her neck, the red-gold strands had begun to dull with age. She was dressed in her usual uniform—a serviceable black skirt and matching waist.

"Where's your apron?" Abigail gave her a hug.

Deborah smoothed a hand over her collar. "I took it off because we have a guest, a new benefactor I'd like you to meet."

"I can't wait to meet him." Abigail's eyebrows rose. "And I've brought another guest with me."

She turned back to the tall, blond minister. "Brother Pierce, this is one of the hardest working women in Natchez, Deborah Trent. She is older sister, mother, and caretaker of all the children here. Deborah, meet Nathan Pierce, our new minister."

They greeted each other as one of the older boys dashed into the house, waved at them, and rushed up the staircase.

Deborah turned from Brother Pierce and frowned toward the young man. "Slow down, Micah. Unless there's a fire upstairs, you need to demonstrate more decorum for the younger children."

"Yes, ma'am." The boy slowed his headlong progress to a trot as he disappeared from sight.

With a smile and a shrug, Deborah led the way into the parlor. "Please excuse me for deserting you, Mr. Ward."

A swarthy stranger stood as they filed into the parlor. The first thing Abigail noticed about him was the mustache he stroked with one long finger. He was well dressed and well groomed, from the careful styling of his dark hair and starched perfection of his shirt collar to the gloss on his black, square-toed boots. All the matrons in town would be pushing their marriageable daughters in his direction.

As Deborah introduced them, Abigail dropped into a reflexive curtsy. He bowed over her hand and pressed a warm kiss on it. The hairs on her arm prickled and she jerked her hand away. She was more accustomed to men kissing the air above her hand.

"It's a pleasure to see you again, Pastor." Mr. Ward's statement made Abigail's jaw drop.

The two men shook hands.

"You two have already met?" Deborah asked the question uppermost in Abigail's mind as she took her place on the horsehair sofa.

Abigail sat on the other end of the sofa and folded her hands in her lap.

"I had no idea how to find your home, so I stepped into the land office to get directions." Brother Pierce explained the circumstances as Deborah poured cups of tea for each of them.

Conversation languished when he finished talking. Abigail sipped her lukewarm tea and wracked her brain for something to ask Mr. Ward about his business in the land office. She glanced in his direction and their gazes clashed. She remembered the way he'd kissed her hand and felt her cheeks warming.

"Mr. Ward has dropped by nearly every day since his arrival last week." Deborah smiled at the man and Abigail breathed a sigh of relief when she felt his gaze move away.

After blotting his mouth and mustache with a linen napkin, Mr. Ward returned his attention to her. "It's the children that I love to see. Their energy and enthusiasm reminds me of my own youth."

"Is that right, Mr. Ward?" Abigail's curiosity blossomed. "Were you an orphan?"

He nodded slowly and steepled his hands under his chin. "My parents died when I was very young, but I was taken in by a distant cousin. If not, I might have been dependent on an establishment like this one." He smiled in her direction. "Of course I once thought orphanages were dreary, harsh places, but since coming to Natchez, I have discovered my mistake. And Miss Trent sings your praises all the time. She tells me you donate large portions of your time here."

"I have not been here nearly as much as I should lately." Abigail balanced her cup and saucer on her knees. "Mama and Papa have kept me busy at home."

"It's always that way during springtime." Deborah smiled at both of the men. "Especially at Magnolia Plantation, since Abigail and her family do not rely on slaves."

"How commendable." Mr. Ward's smile was directed toward her. "My cousin and I have never agreed with slavery."

Perhaps Mr. Ward deserved more consideration. "I've never understood why so many think slavery is necessary. Papa has never relied on slaves. The moment he purchased Magnolia, he freed all the people there and offered to help them get established on their own farms. We pay living wages to our help, and Magnolia still prospers."

Abigail looked toward Brother Pierce. His gaze seemed focused on the tea in his cup. But then he glanced up. His expression was cloaked, his mouth forming a straight line as he studied her. She straightened her posture, a defensive reaction.

"I only wish more plantation owners agreed with you and your father." Mr. Ward's comment drew her attention away from the noncommittal pastor. "Perhaps others will follow your lead."

Her heart warmed at his supportive words. Abigail smiled at Mr. Ward. "We can only pray for that result."

Deborah stirred a lump of sugar into her tea and leaned forward. "Very true. I have always admired your parents' stand on abolition. And that of your great-aunt and great-uncle. They freed all of the slaves at Tanner Plantation after your parents proved it was possible. Who can say what effect their successful operations will have on other planters? Perhaps one day all of Natchez will turn from slavery."

"I am amazed to find such heartfelt abolitionist leanings here." Brother Pierce entered the conversation. "Before coming to Natchez, I had believed everyone here supported slavery. In eastern Tennessee, slavery is almost nonexistent. The people work their own farms. But of course, we do not have such massive operations as here."

Abigail looked at him out of the corner of her eye. Was that why he had no firm opinion on such matters? Perhaps she should not be so quick to judge him. If she traveled to Chattanooga, she would surely run into many things that were different. Things she had no opinion about because she didn't have enough information. Shame pricked her. But slavery? Should that be condoned in any circumstance? She didn't think so. Perhaps it was time to change the subject to something less contentious. "What's new here? It seems so long since I came by."

"As a matter of fact, before you arrived Mr. Ward and I were discussing a rather strange occurrence. I don't know exactly what to make of it." Deborah put her spoon on the service tray, and a small frown drew her eyebrows together. "I don't believe in such things, but some of the children have become convinced we have a ghost."

The hairs on the back of Abigail's neck lifted. "A ghost?" She looked from her friend to the newcomer. Both were nodding. "Are you sure it's not a jest?"

"Oh no." Deborah's frown deepened. "A couple of nights ago, several of the girls came screaming out of their bedroom. They were terrified."

"Exactly what frightened them?"

"One of the girls was awakened by a noise. She's frightened of mice and thought that was what she was hearing. She woke up another girl, and they got out of their beds to investigate. Both of them saw a weird green light shining under the door. Their screams woke the others, and they stampeded from the room en masse."

Brother Pierce shifted in his chair. "Who was in the hallway?"

"No one."

Deborah's quiet words made Abigail's eyes widen. She could feel her discomfort increasing with every second ticking by. "What do you suppose it was?"

A shrug answered her question. "I hope it was nothing more than a bad dream and a vivid imagination. I don't like the idea of someone wandering around the house at night."

"Perhaps you should contact the sheriff." Brother Pierce's voice was gentle and restored Abigail's equilibrium.

"That's a good idea." She reached over and patted Deborah's hand. "I can stop by his office on my way home."

"Thank you for your concern, but I don't really think it's necessary." Deborah squeezed Abigail's hand. "But I promise to contact him myself if anything else happens. I will not put the children in danger."

Mr. Ward cleared his throat. "I think you have the right idea, Miss Trent. But you must not forget to contact the authorities if you have any further trouble."

Abigail put her teacup back on the serving tray and stood up. "I suppose we should get back to Magnolia."

The other three also stood. After saying good-bye and promising to come back soon, Abigail and Brother Pierce left the large house. As they walked across the front lawn, she glanced up at the tall man. "You are a man of surprises."

He settled his hat on his head. "What do you mean?"

"I am amazed you have met both Mia and Mr. Ward."

A slow chuckle rumbled through his chest. "It was a matter of happenstance. The little girl found me. She seems to have confused me with her uncle."

"Yes, it is very sad. Mia lost all of her family. We have sent out inquiries for grandparents or cousins but no one has answered them. But she doesn't usually show such affection to strangers. You must have made quite an impression on her."

"I don't know about that." He opened the gate for her.

Abigail waited as he latched it behind them. She could see why the little girl might be attracted to him. Brother Pierce was nothing like most pastors she had met. He was methodical and quiet, a man one could rely upon. She wondered if he was quiet when he preached, too. That would be a change. Most of the pastors in this part of the world were fiery and loud when they took the pulpit. It would be interesting to listen to his sermons.

On the ride back to Magnolia Plantation, Abigail pointed out some of the larger plantations and told him the story of how her father had come to Natchez from New Orleans. She loved the story of his bringing Mr. Hughes home after the battle against the British at New Orleans. He was a good listener, easy to talk to because of the interested questions he asked about those times. By the time they turned into the winding lane that led to the plantation house, she was feeling much more kindly toward him. "Please make plans to dine with us again this evening."

His blue eyes studied her so long that Abigail began to wonder if her hat was askew. She resisted the urge to check and waited for his answer.

"I do appreciate the invitation, Miss LeGrand, but I must refuse. I have several chores that must be completed. Letters and unpacking and such. Please give my regrets to your estimable parents."

The sting of his refusal made her cheeks burn. With a curt nod, she turned her horse's head and cantered away. Abigail knew she shouldn't care if he would rather eat alone than join her at the family dinner table. So why did she?

six

"Thank you for giving me a ride to the church." A drop of water slipped down Nathan's back, and he wondered if the dreary weather was a statement from God about his sermon.

"It's no trouble at all." Mrs. LeGrand smiled at him.

Mr. LeGrand tucked his wife's hand under his elbow. "We didn't want you to arrive drenched."

"At least the worst of the storm has passed." Sitting to his right, Abigail was the picture of spring. Her dress was as green as spring leaves, and her perfume tantalized him. Sweet with a hint of spice. Nathan wanted to savor the scent. She was so pretty, and this morning she was the picture of maidenly innocence. He wondered why she had not been snapped up by some handsome, rich swain. Perhaps all the men in this part of the world were blind. . .or more likely intimidated by her intelligence and independent spirit.

If he was looking for a wife, she would be the perfect candidate. Of course he was not. The last thing he wanted was to fall in love and marry. He had more important tasks to complete. And he never wanted to be in the position of again having to use his physical strength against a human being. He shuddered.

"Are you cold, Pastor?" Abigail looked over at him.

Prickles of heat broke out on his forehead. "No, I was thinking of something." He hoped none of the other occupants could see how hot he had grown.

Mr. LeGrand glanced his way. "You don't need to be nervous about your sermon, Brother Pierce."

"That's right." Mrs. LeGrand leaned forward and patted his knee.

Her motherly concern wrapped him in a cocoon. It had been so long since anyone fussed over him. He hadn't realized the lack until this very minute. Since the death of his aunt a decade earlier, he and his uncle had lived without a caring, feminine touch.

The coach lurched through a rut, and Abigail fell against him. "I'm sorry."

Their bodies were pressed together from knee to shoulder. Her hair tickled his nose, and her perfume filled his senses. Part of him wanted the contact to linger, but he helped her sit back up. "It wasn't your fault."

For the rest of the trip to town, he listened to Mr. LeGrand talk about the effect today's rain would have on crops. The older man obviously loved growing things. But Nathan found it hard to concentrate on the fine points of germination and cultivation. His mind was still preoccupied with the past. And the fateful night when everything changed. His hand jerked as for a brief instant he relived the feel of the sharp knife sliding into another man's body.

"Are you okay?" Abigail's concerned gaze combed his face. "You look pale."

He cleared his throat and straightened his shoulders. "I'm fine. I'm trying to get my thoughts in order."

"I'm sure you'll do a wonderful job."

Nathan appreciated her kindness and the supportive nods of her parents. But as the carriage drew up to the church, he wondered if he had made a terrible mistake to become a pastor. What did he know of such things? He was as guilty as anyone else.

They entered the church to find it only half full. But that didn't stop Mrs. LeGrand from introducing him to everyone who had preceded them. The first couple was Mr. and Mrs. Hughes, the managers of Natchez's most successful shipping business. The second couple, Mr. and Mrs. Sheffield, were not as welcoming. He suspected there might be an interesting story behind their attitudes.

He renewed his acquaintance with Abigail's great-aunt and great-uncle whom he had first met at the waterfront mission. Several other couples and families went out of their way to make him feel welcome.

By the time he began the sermon, his trepidation had eased. He retold the story of Noah, a man who had listened to God's whispers and ignored the opinions of his neighbors. He warned them to focus on the world to come and reminded them that they were all sojourners in this world. Then he concluded by reading to them from Paul's epistle to the Philippians: " 'For to me to live is Christ, and to die is gain.'"

When he stepped down from the pulpit, the townspeople crowded around him. He received their congratulations with a feeling of accomplishment. He had survived the first sermon in his circuit.

"That was a wonderful sermon, Brother Pierce." Somehow he heard her voice above all the other people in the church.

"Thank you, Miss LeGrand. I'm pleased you enjoyed it."

"Yes, Brother Pierce." Her father clapped him on the back. "You have the makings of a fine pastor. I can see why you were chosen to be a circuit rider. God is going to use you in a very powerful way."

Nathan ducked his head. He wasn't sure if the older man's words were true or not, nor was he certain he wanted to be used in a powerful way. He'd rather serve God quietly, pay for his sins, and maybe make a difference in a few people's lives. He had no desire to set the world on fire.

"Come, come." Mrs. LeGrand's voice interrupted his thoughts. "I've been telling everyone about the ball we'll be having in a week to make certain you get the chance to meet everyone."

"A ball?" The words struck terror in his heart. "I don't know if that's a good idea."

Mrs. LeGrand put a hand on his arm. "Of course it's a good idea. Wait and see. Everyone in the county will attend. It will be a great deal of fun. And you can dance with all the pretty girls. A handsome man like you, and one with such a commanding air, all the girls will be eager to have you partner with them. And who knows? Perhaps we'll even manage to find you someone special. Someone you can spend the rest of your life with."

Feeling like a leaf caught in a maelstrom, he followed her back out of the church. Surely there would be a way to halt her matchmaking plans. The last thing he needed was a wife.

seven

"Abigail, you look lovelier than usual this evening." Her father beamed as he watched her descend the central staircase. "You'll be the belle of the ball."

She rolled her eyes as she reached the first floor. "There will be a dozen young ladies who have a better claim to that title than I."

Papa hugged her and dropped a kiss on her cheek. "They cannot begin to compare." He stepped back. "Is that a new dress?"

"Oh, Papa. Of course it's not new." She laughed. "I've been much too busy to go for a fitting."

Her mother joined them. "Sometimes I wonder if you keep yourself so busy so you can avoid having a family of your own."

Abigail had heard this speech before. She dropped a curtsy. "I'm trying to emulate you, Mama. Remember telling me how close you once came to marrying the wrong man?"

"Twice." Papa winked at her. "She didn't tell you about the soldier she met in New Orleans."

Wrinkling her brow in confusion, Abigail turned to her mother. "I thought you were engaged for a short time to Lowell Sheffield because your family pushed you to marry."

Her mother cleared her throat. "Yes, but that was a couple of years later."

"Wait, I have to hear this story. You met someone in New Orleans?"

Was that a flush in her mother's cheeks?

Abigail's head swiveled back to her father. "Weren't you a soldier in New Orleans?"

"Yes, but I wasn't the type to spend my nights at the local balls, so sadly, I never met your mother until I moved here."

She couldn't believe her mother had never told her about falling in love with a soldier. Was she still in love with him? Or had Papa turned her head? "Who was he?"

Her mother put her hands on her hips. "He's no one important. I once fancied myself interested in Asher Landon because I thought we could make an advantageous match. But he was in love with someone else. And I thank God for that. If he had not given me the cold shoulder, I might never have come home to Natchez. And I might never have met your papa."

"And then I would have spent my life alone." Her father put an arm around her mother's waist and hugged her briefly.

The front knocker sounded, and he relinquished his hold to answer the door. Abigail stood next to her mother as their guests arrived, her mind captivated by the glimpse into her parents' past. She tried to imagine them young and in love, but it was beyond her ability.

A pang of some emotion tightened her chest. She was determined to remain single until God arranged for her to meet the right man, someone who would not try to curtail her dreams. He would have to live here with her in Natchez so she could continue helping at the orphanage and working in the waterfront mission. He would be accommodating and thoughtful, a man who listened to her ideas and supported her efforts—

Brother Pierce stepped into the foyer, and her galloping thoughts came to a sudden halt. While he shook hands with her father and bowed to her mother, Abigail reached a hand up to check her coiffure even though she knew it was secure. Jemma had outdone herself, winding Abigail's long hair into dips and swirls and securing it with ribbons and diamond-studded pins. And although her dress was not new, it was one of her favorites, made of pale pink jonquil, with deep flounces and wide sleeves. She liked the way it swirled around her ankles as she danced.

"You're looking especially lovely this evening, Miss LeGrand." Brother Pierce took her outstretched hand in his own.

The light reflected off of his thick hair, like molten gold, as he bowed. Her heart stuttered as his large fingers squeezed her hand gently before straightening. "Th–thank you, sir. I...It..." Why wouldn't her mouth work properly? She took a quick breath and prayed to regain her composure. "We haven't seen you much this week."

"I have been preparing for my first trip to some of the surrounding areas."

A feeling not unlike emptiness filled the pit of her stomach. He was leaving? "How long will you be gone?"

He shrugged. "I don't really know. I have met with my predecessor several times this week. He says he generally spent ten days to two weeks on the circuit, but he suggested I curtail this trek and return in time for Sunday services."

Abigail realized her shoulders had drooped at some time in their conversation. She straightened them with an effort and forced her mouth up in a smile. She was not some young girl to moon over the handsome pastor. "Then I'll wish you Godspeed."

He nodded and turned to go into the ballroom.

Even as she greeted other guests, she had a difficult time concentrating on their conversations, her gaze often straying to the people in the ballroom as though she was trying to catch a glimpse of a certain tall, blond minister.

When her parents deemed it time, they joined the others. As soon as she entered the ballroom, Silas Ward stepped forward. Had he been watching for her?

His dark eyes glowed in the light of the chandelier. "You look so beautiful this evening. The color of your apparel is only eclipsed by the bloom of your cheeks."

Raising an eyebrow at his effusiveness, Abigail looked past his right shoulder and met Brother Pierce's serious gaze. "Thank you, Mr. Ward. You are most kind. I trust you are making yourself at home in our busy town."

"Yes, yes. Natchez is a beautiful and interesting town. From the muddy banks and saloons of Under-the-Hill to the stately mansions like your home, I have found this town to be welcoming." He stroked his mustache.

"I'm glad you like our little piece of the world. Things are not perfect in Natchez, not by any means. But for the most part, all of these people have their redeeming qualities."

She turned to slip past him, but Mr. Ward put a hand on her arm. "I was wondering if you would honor me with a dance."

Although she had planned to make a quick round of the people in the room, she could not resist the plea in his dark brown eyes. "Yes, of course, Mr. Ward."

As if on cue, the musicians began playing a waltz. Mr. Ward held out an arm and escorted her to the center of the room. His arm went around her waist, and Abigail assumed the proper position as he swept her into the dance. At first she found it a little difficult to follow his lead, but then the music caught her. Abigail forgot the awkwardness and allowed him to twirl her around the room to the strains of Johann Strauss's "Viennese Carnival."

"I have not seen you at the orphanage this week." His voice tickled her ear.

Abigail pulled away a little. "I generally go by there in the morning. Deborah always needs help with the youngest children while she is teaching the others reading and arithmetic."

"I see. Perhaps I should make it a habit to drop by and help you."

She concentrated on the lapel of his coat. "I'm not certain that's a good idea. Deborah has been telling me how much she appreciates your afternoon visits. She says you are very good with the older boys."

"I don't do much."

She could not fault his modesty. Deborah said Silas had been teaching the boys how to whittle. "At least what you're teaching them will keep them occupied and out of trouble. At best they could learn skills for future employment." Abigail glanced up at his face, surprised to see that his cheeks had flushed. "I hope I have not spoken out of turn."

His hand tightened around her waist. "Of course not. I appreciate your compliments. I would be quite disturbed if I thought you did not approve of my feeble efforts to make a difference. Those poor boys. At the risk of losing your good opinion, I must admit that their circumstances disturb me greatly."

Her eyebrows climbed up toward her scalp. She stiffened in his arms. "Are you saying Deborah's not doing a good job?"

"Oh no." His jaw dropped open. "That's not what I meant at all. In fact, the orphanage is exemplary. And Miss Trent is a capable matron. If all orphanages were as well run as this one, our world would be a much happier place."

The waltz drew to a close, and Abigail stepped away from him. "I enjoyed our dance, Mr. Ward, but I fear I must leave you to attend my duties as hostess."

He bowed. "Of course. But I hope to speak with you again on this matter. I cannot have you thinking I do not approve of the orphanage."

"That's not necessary, Mr. Ward. You have explained yourself quite admirably. I appreciate your kindness to the children and your compliments concerning Miss Trent." She felt his gaze on her as she crossed the room and could not decide if she liked the attention or not.

Charlotte Thornton stood next to her mother, Susannah Hughes, and Abigail's mother. She joined them and spent the next hour listening to their discussion of the trials and joys of motherhood. Charlotte had a way of giving a humorous bent to her children's escapades. Soon they were all laughing as she described her daughter's attempts to whistle back at a yellow warbler perched on a tree near her bedroom window.

Standing with her back to the ballroom, Abigail felt rather than saw someone standing close to her. She turned and almost buried her nose in a starched shirt. Her breath caught as she looked up into the new minister's blue gaze. His eyes reminded her of summertime—long, warm afternoons spent rocking in the shade of the front porch and watching the boats pass by on the ribbon of river at the base of their bluff. Heat from her memories might be the reason her cheeks were so flushed.

"Can I tear you away from your friends long enough for a dance?"

"She would love to dance with you, Brother Pierce." Her mother answered his question for her.

It wasn't that she didn't want to dance with him. The problem was feeling as though she was being pushed in that direction. Abigail held herself stiffly during the opening bars of yet another waltz. Did this orchestra know any other types of songs?

"Thank you for agreeing to dance with me, Miss LeGrand."

"The honor is mine, Brother Pierce." She gave the acceptable response although what she really wanted to do was slip away. How dare her mother put her in this predicament. Brother Pierce probably thought she was desperate for a husband. Bad enough that every time he showed up her tongue tied itself in knots.

He cleared his throat, causing her to look up into his eyes once more. The whole room seemed to disappear around her as she fell into their blue depths. Why did his eyes have to be such an arresting color?

"I wish you would not call me Brother Pierce." He smiled

down at her, and the blue color deepened. "It makes me feel so old. . .and responsible for giving the right answer all of the time."

Abigail's heart melted at the vulnerability exposed by his words. She had never considered what it might mean to be a pastor. Of course she knew he would have to prepare sermons and visit the sick. Her mind went back to the days when she was a child and the pastor visited. Her parents had turned to him for reassurance and advice on any number of topics. Sometimes they had even sent her from the room so she would not be privy to the more adult problems they faced. "All right, Nathan. But I have a couple of conditions."

"What conditions?" His smile wavered.

"First, you must call me Abigail."

He nodded. "Agreed, Abigail."

"And the second is that you must help me at the orphanage whenever you are in town."

He hesitated a moment and almost stumbled. "I suppose so."

"Good. Strange things are occurring there, and Deborah and I would like to talk to someone about them."

The music stopped before she could elaborate further. He escorted her back to her mother. "I don't know if I'll see you before I leave tomorrow, Abigail, Mrs. LeGrand. But please rest assured you will all be in my prayers."

"That's very kind of you, Nathan." She could feel her mother's approving glance on her as he strode across the room. How would she ever explain their conversation without raising her parents' hopes?

Maybe it had been a bad idea to agree to Nathan's request. But how could she have refused the plea in those piercing blue eyes of his? The answer was simple. She couldn't.

eight

"I really enjoyed your preaching, Brother Pierce." The woman's gap-toothed grin reminded Nathan of the jack-o'-lanterns he had carved as a child. "We been needing a good preaching. There's folk here what turned from God and is going to burn in hell when they die."

He was sure her words were meant to encourage him, but they had the opposite effect. He felt the weight of responsibility settle firmly on his shoulders. If he was not effective in explaining God's Word, others would pay the ultimate price. "Thank you, ma'am."

A sigh filled him before he turned his attention to the last few people waiting to greet him. Doubt seemed to chase after him each day on his circuit. Was he doing the right thing? Was he bringing converts into the fold? Was he good enough to preach God's message of salvation and forgiveness? If he told these people what he'd done, would they turn from him in shock and disgust? He didn't know the answers to the questions that dogged him. And no matter how hard he prayed for answers, God remained stubbornly silent.

The day was growing warm, and his coat was beginning to itch. Nathan promised himself a quick bath in the nearby stream before getting back on his horse and heading for the next town. But before he could enjoy that, he would have to see what these people needed. He smiled at the couple, a man about his own age and a pretty young woman who looked about five years younger. "What can I do for you?"

The man rolled the brim of his hat between his hands as though he was nervous. "We. . .uh. . .we was hoping you could marry us, Preacher. We been waiting for someone to come by who could say the words over us and make everything all legal-like. My name's Frank Horton and this is Abigail, the woman I love more'n anything."

Of course she looked nothing like the LeGrands' daughter, but Nathan couldn't stop his mind from conjuring up a picture of the engaging woman he'd danced with on his last evening in Natchez. The girl in front of him was dressed in a plain shift that had been mended many times. Her eye color was much lighter than his Abigail's ebony gaze.

His thoughts halted. *His Abigail?* Where had that come from? Abigail LeGrand did not belong to anyone, least of all a traveling preacher with a shameful past.

He dragged his wandering thoughts back to the couple. "I would be happy to do so." He smiled at them, opened his *Book of Common Prayer.* " 'Dearly beloved: We have come together. . .' " The words flowed around them, timeless and wonderful.

When he finished, he closed his eyes and bowed his head, waiting a moment to make sure the couple followed his lead. "Lord, here I stand next to Frank and Abigail, who present themselves humbly before You and ask that You bless their union. They have deep feelings of commitment and love for each other and pledge that they will always cling to You first and each other second. Please guide and direct them, keep their hearts tender one to the other, and may their union bring glory and honor to Your name above all else. In the name of Your precious Son, Jesus, the one who died so that all of us might have eternal life, amen."

"Amen and thank you, Preacher." The man put his crumpled hat back on his head and shook Nathan's hand with enthusiasm before turning back to Abigail. "I guess we need to get back to your ma's house. She's gonna need you to help with the young'uns."

Nathan walked with them to the edge of the meadow,

where he'd tethered his horse. "I'll stop in at the county courthouse on my way out of town and ask them to record your names."

They nodded and thanked him once again before walking away hand-in-hand. He watched them for a moment, surprised by the yearning in his heart as Frank pulled his new bride close and planted a gentle kiss on her cheek.

What would it feel like to fall in love and marry? He had once believed he loved Iris Landon, and he had even wondered if he loved Margaret Coleridge. But that had been before he murdered a man. The stain on his soul because of that terrible deed would likely prevent him from ever really falling in love. And it would certainly stop any self-respecting young lady from wanting to marry him.

Nathan tucked his Bible into his saddlebag and removed his coat. The sooner he got that through his thick skull, the better. Maybe soaking it in the creek would help clear his head. He certainly hoped so.

&

"It must be here somewhere." Abigail could hear the frustration in Deborah's voice.

She put a hand on her friend's shoulder. "Don't worry, we're going to find it. It's probably been mislaid."

Having arrived at the orphanage late, Abigail had been surprised to find the children barely controlled by Sheba, the young black woman who cooked and helped care for the orphans. Deborah, she had explained, wouldn't come out of her bedroom.

Concerned that the capable administrator was sick, Abigail had gone upstairs and found a scene of chaos in Deborah's usually orderly room. The rocking chair had been pushed away from its corner, the padded cushion dangling from one corner of the seat. Blankets and pillows made a pile next to the bureau. Clothing hung haphazardly from the drawers suspended at precarious angles, and Deborah's water pitcher and bowl were upside down. The hand-knotted rug Abigail had helped her make had been rolled up and leaned against the wall between the pair of windows overlooking the street. Even the drapes had not been spared—they had been pulled down and now lay in heaps like discarded rags.

"I know I'm being silly about an inexpensive piece of gaudy jewelry, but that bracelet is the only reminder I have of my mother. It has no intrinsic value. I know I left it somewhere in my room last Sunday after the service." The distraught woman jerked the drawer out of the bureau and dumped the entire contents on the bed, grunting with the effort.

Abigail helped her comb through gloves, handkerchiefs, and cotton pantaloons. Something glimmered in the light from the window. "Is that it?"

"Where?" Deborah pounced at the spot Abigail indicated. "No." She lifted a shiny button up. "This came off of my walking dress and I have not had time to sew it back on."

"Your bracelet doesn't seem to be in here." Abigail surveyed the bedroom. She had never seen Deborah's room in such a state of chaos. "Perhaps you laid it down somewhere else because one of the children interrupted you. Wait and see. As soon as we discover it, you will remember what happened."

Deborah tossed the contents back into the drawer without folding them. "I hope you're right."

After helping her slide the drawer back into the bureau, Abigail sat down on the rumpled bed. "Have you looked anywhere else?"

"No, I cannot imagine it would be anywhere else. I always send the children up to change out of their Sunday clothes, and I do the same. That's when I take the bracelet off and put it away." Deborah covered her face with her hands.

Abigail got up and put her arms around the distraught woman. She pushed back her concern about finding the bracelet. Now was not the time to voice her doubt. Deborah needed comfort. "Never fear. We will find it if it's anywhere in the house. Have you talked to Sheba? Maybe she has seen it."

Deborah shook her head. "I have not said anything about it. I'm sure they wonder if I've lost my senses, but I'd rather they think that than to feel accused of thievery."

"Only a guilty conscience would make someone feel accused." Abigail squeezed Deborah's shoulders before stepping back and pointing to the bed. "Why don't you sit down over there while I straighten up the room a little? Who knows? Maybe I'll find the bracelet as I put your things away."

She bustled about putting order to the room while Deborah followed her suggestion. As she worked, Abigail tried to come up with other locations where her friend might have left the bracelet, but every suggestion she made was answered with a breathy no or a shake of the head. By the time she finished tidying the room, her list of possibilities had been exhausted.

"I don't see any way around asking the others if they have seen your jewelry. I understand your reservations, but it must be done." She perched beside Deborah and handed her a handkerchief. "Would you rather I asked? That way you can place the blame on me if anyone's feelings are bruised."

"No, I'll do it." Deborah scrubbed at her face with the square of lace. "I had to make sure it wasn't in here first. In all the years I've been here, nothing has ever been stolen. But I suppose I'm going to have to face facts. Someone in this house is a thief."

"Let's not jump to conclusions. I am still hoping we will find it in the kitchen or lying on the hall table." She met Deborah's forlorn gaze with a smile she hoped was comforting. "Let's check, and if we do not find it, we'll move forward from there."

The children were finishing their breakfast as the two women went downstairs and looked around for the piece of jewelry. When they still could not find it, they called the children and Sheba together and explained what had happened. Being very careful to avoid accusing anyone, Deborah asked if her bracelet had been seen. Worried stares and shakes of the head answered her. No one knew where it could be.

"I'll bet the ghost took it," said one of the older boys.

Fear radiated from the younger children, and even one or two of the older ones looked over their shoulders or shuffled their feet.

"Don't be silly." Abigail stood up to get their attention. "Ghosts don't exist."

Mia nodded her head. "Yes, they do. We hear them at night, Miss Abigail. They pull chains around in the attic and moan like the wind."

"And they walk around in the halls sometimes," another girl added in solemn tones. "But I hide under my covers so they won't see me and take me away."

A little boy began to cry at her gloomy words.

Deborah clapped her hands. "That's enough. All of you know better than to frighten each other. We are a family in this house, and families don't scare each other with tales of imaginary spirits." She opened her arms to the little boy who was crying. He ran to her and buried his head against her shoulder. "Don't worry, Timmy. Everything's going to be all right." She gathered him up and walked out of the parlor, murmuring comforting words in his ear.

Abigail frowned at the older children. "Miss Deborah's bracelet is the thing we need to worry about. I want each of you to keep a sharp eye out for it. As for the other matter, when we find out what is making all the odd noises, some of you are going to feel quite foolish that you let yourselves be tricked into believing such nonsense."

Sheba had not said anything during the meeting, but as the scolded children began to file out of the room, she came to where Abigail stood. "I don't hear those sounds on account of I go home at night, Miss Abigail, but the children sure do talk about it a lot. And I'm wondering now if it's not some homeless varmint hiding out up there and coming down when he thinks it is safe."

Abigail rested her chin on one finger as she considered the maid's words. "Do you think it's a runaway?"

Sheba shrugged. "I don't know about that, but it wouldn't surprise me none."

"Perhaps I need to have Papa and some of the men from the plantation come over here and check it out. If it is a runaway, they'll help the poor soul get away safely."

"And if it's not?" Sheba's eyes grew wide as she voiced the question.

Abigail dropped her hand to her hip. "No matter who it is, I'm sure Papa can take care of it." She infused her voice with all the confidence she could muster. It would not help anyone to see how doubtful she really felt.

≈

"Squirrels?" Abigail could not keep the disbelief out of her voice.

Her father had gone to town this morning to check on the orphanage while she and her mother stayed home to wash linens. She would have much preferred to go with him, but she had not been able to desert her mother. After hours stirring heavy sheets with a long stick, she was more than willing to take a break and listen to her father's report.

"That's right." Her father nodded his head for emphasis. "We found two nests in the attic, so I can understand why the children heard noises."

"How did they get inside the orphanage?"

"They're crafty animals." He frowned. "It doesn't take much of an opening. And they can do a great deal of damage once they manage to get inside."

"How will you make certain they don't come back?"

"That's easy. Susannah Hughes told me last week that her

cat has weaned a litter of kittens. I sent her a message to send one over to the orphanage." His chuckle drew an answering smile from her. "I think that will be one well-groomed cat if the children have anything to say about it."

Her mother came back from the clothesline with an empty basket. "What are you two laughing about?"

"Cats and squirrels." Her father caught his wife up in a hug and swung her around. The basket slipped out of her hands and bounced toward the back porch. He explained about his morning discoveries as he dropped a series of quick kisses from her ear to her mouth.

Abigail rolled her eyes at her parents' antics. "You two act more like newlyweds than a staid, married couple."

"It's your papa's fault." Her mother giggled as the man holding her pressed one last kiss on the back of her neck. "He shouldn't be such a romantic man."

"And your mama shouldn't be so beautiful."

"Okay, okay." Abigail put her hands on her hips. "Papa, can you quit nuzzling my mother long enough to tell me if you found Deborah's bracelet?"

Mama's cheeks were flushed. When Papa released her, she rescued the laundry basket and turned to face him.

He sighed and shook his head. "No, we didn't. And I must say squirrels don't usually show interest in shiny objects. That would be more like a bird, although I can't imagine a bird strong enough to fly off with a piece as large as a bracelet."

"That's too bad." Her mother pulled a sheet from the rinse water and wrung it out. "Maybe we can find one like it to give to Deborah."

"I don't know." Abigail returned to her stirring. "It belonged to her mother. We'll have to keep praying it will turn up. I cannot believe anyone at the orphanage would take it."

"It's beginning to look like that's the only reasonable explanation." Her father leaned against a tree and watched them work. "But perhaps it will show up yet."

Mama dropped the sheet into her basket and grabbed another one. "You could help us instead of watching."

"I believe that's my cue to check on the stables." Papa pushed himself away from the tree and sauntered away. "You two seem to have the wash well in hand."

Abigail didn't even try to hide her snort. "So much for togetherness."

She and her mother continued working with Jemma until all the wash was hanging on the clothesline. They would have to come back out before dusk to bring the dry linens in for ironing tomorrow. At least that job wouldn't make her eyes water like the lye fumes had this morning. And climbing into a bed of fresh linens tomorrow night would be worth all of their hard work.

nine

Coming back to the cottage at Magnolia already felt like coming home. Nathan knew how lucky he was to have such a luxurious place to live in. Most traveling pastors had little besides a bedroll and a Bible.

Early morning sunlight cascaded onto the marble floor as he walked through the foyer. After a week on the road, he should have been able to stay abed this morning, but the birdsong outside his window had called to him.

He rubbed his chin as he walked along the shaded path toward the bluff overlooking the Mississippi River. Perhaps he should have taken the time to shave, but he had wanted to enjoy the morning before anyone else was up. His destination this morning was a large wooden bench on the LeGrands' front lawn that commanded a wide view of the river. Mr. and Mrs. LeGrand talked about enjoying the sunset from the bench, but he wanted to enjoy the vista as the day awoke. Following the pathway, he caught a glimpse of a yearling picking its way through the undergrowth some distance away.

He emerged from the pathway onto the grounds and took a moment to study the plantation home. It was a graceful building with tall white columns and a deep porch that faced the river. In front of the house, old oak trees stood watch over a small pond, whose surface rippled under the invisible brush of a spring breeze. He wondered if Abigail had ever waded at the water's edge or attempted to climb the gnarled limbs of the overhanging trees. It wasn't hard to imagine her being so daring.

Turning to the bench, he was surprised to see it was already occupied. Who else had been called out so early? His eyes narrowed as he tried to make out the person's identity. He did not want to bother anyone, but his curiosity took him several steps closer. A woman. Abigail. Something was wrong. She sat hunched forward, her shoulders shaking and her head in her hands. Was she crying? Concern propelled Nathan forward. "Are you okay?"

Her head jerked upward and that's when he realized her hair was loose as it flew around her. "What are you doing here?" A white towel fluttered to the ground.

"I'm sorry. I didn't mean to startle you, Abigail." He realized his mistake when he searched her face for signs of tears. "I saw you sitting here and I thought you might be in distress and need someone to talk to."

"Distress?" She reached back with both hands and grabbed her hair, struggling to keep it under control. "You frightened me out of my wits. Yes, I'm stressed. You've caught me practically undressed."

At first he thought she was really upset, and his chest tightened in response. He opened his mouth to apologize yet again, but then he saw the gleam in her midnight black eyes. She was teasing him. His chest eased and a smile turned up the corners of his mouth. "Don't put it up on my account."

She stopped trying to twist the damp strands into a bun. "I suppose you will think I am some kind of wanton female, but I washed it this morning and decided to sit out here and let the wind blow it dry." As soon as she let go of the bundle, it fell down again around her shoulders. "I cannot abide the fragrance of lye soap, so I always wash my hair after Mama and I launder the linens."

Nathan took a deep breath to still the sudden pounding of his heart. She looked so vulnerable standing on the far side of the bench. He pushed aside the longing that crept into him. He had no business thinking about running his fingers through her soft tresses. Only her husband would have that right.

Abigail did not seem aware of the effect she was having on him. She beckoned him forward and sat down once more facing the bluff. "I didn't realize you had returned."

Instead of sitting next to her, he leaned against the trunk of a pine tree that stood next to her bench. "I came in yesterday evening."

"I trust your trip was successful." She turned her dark gaze on him. "Did you win more hearts for the Lord?"

He shook his head. "I cannot take credit. I am only a laborer in the field. Jesus is the one who harvests."

"Well said, Nathan. All of us should share your humility." She glanced up at him. "It is one of your most admirable traits."

She thought he had admirable traits? Nathan wanted to ask her to list them, but he supposed that would contradict the humility she attributed to him. He glanced to the river, watching as a flatboat cut an angle across the wide bend below them. Perhaps he would do better to focus on her. "What has been going on here since my departure?"

"Much the same as what was happening while you were here." She brushed at a pine straw that had landed on the bench next to her. "Although we have solved the mystery of the odd sounds at the orphanage."

"Is that so?" Nathan looked back toward her. As she explained about squirrels and kittens he watched the expressions cross her face. The more he was around Abigail LeGrand, the more he found to admire about her. Strong and courageous, she was the type of woman who would meet all of life's challenges with a resolute spirit.

He wondered about the source of her strength. Was it because she had grown up in the lap of luxury? That did not make sense to him. Most people who grew up that way became self-absorbed boors with no idea that they should work on behalf of others.

Which led him back to his question—from where did she

draw her strength? Her values? One thing was for certain—her contradictions intrigued him. He had never met anyone like Abigail LeGrand.

⁂

Abigail straightened and looked across the strawberry patch, where she and her mother were working once again. They had already gathered some of the succulent fruits a few weeks earlier, and this would likely be their last harvest for this year. "You're supposed to pick the berries, not eat all of them, Mama."

Her mother's guilty look made Abigail laugh out loud. "Did you think I wouldn't see you?"

"They're too sweet for me to resist." Mama pulled her bonnet forward and bent to gather more of the red fruit.

Abigail dropped another handful into her basket, palming one to pop into her mouth. "You make an excellent point."

Laughter filled the air.

"I think we have enough for now." Mama started for the kitchen, her basket piled high.

Abigail grabbed her basket with both hands and followed. "I saw a new recipe in the *Natchez Free Trader* last week."

"Was it a cake recipe?" The older woman emptied her basket into a vat of water that had been drawn earlier. "I think I remember seeing it."

"We also need to make some preserves. I love strawberry preserves on your fresh bread."

"That's a wonderful idea, daughter. We'll take it with us on our trip."

Abigail removed her bonnet. "What trip?"

"A big church conference is going to be held in Jackson in two weeks, and your papa and I have decided to go."

"I thought we were going to Gatlin's Camp Ground like last year." Abigail was shocked at her mother's pronouncement. Her parents usually consulted her before making their plans. It wasn't that she had anything against traveling to the capital city. She had never visited Jackson before.

"We'll probably go there, too." Mama swirled the strawberries vigorously enough to wash them clean. "But we thought it would be nice to visit with the elders in Jackson. We were also thinking about asking Brother Pierce to travel with us."

Abigail's mouth dropped open. "Why would you want to do that? We never took Brother Harris with us to Gatlin's Camp Ground when he was the pastor, much less to Jackson."

A secret smile teased her mother's lips. "But this is a different situation."

"Mamaaa." She drew out the last syllable to indicate her objection to the idea. "You have got to stop interfering in my life. I am not interested in Nath—Brother Pierce. And he's not interested in me."

Her mother put down the spoon and rested her hands on her hips. "Abigail, I love you dearly, but you have got to realize that not everything going on in this household revolves around you."

The words struck home. She sat down hard in a convenient rocking chair. "I didn't. . ."

Mama leaned over her and put a hand on Abigail's cheek. "I'm sorry, dear. But you are jumping to the wrong conclusion. We were thinking about Brother Pierce. He's all alone and new to the area. If he doesn't go with us, he'd likely have to go by horseback and sleep out in the open. This way, he can go with us on the steamship to Vicksburg and then overland on the stagecoach to Jackson."

"Have you talked to Brother Pierce about your plans?" Abigail got up from the rocker and started pulling strawberries from the water and capping them with a sharp knife.

"Now when would I have talked to Brother Pierce? Your pa and I only decided that we'd make the trip a few days ago, and he hasn't returned from his circuit." Her mother glanced at her for a moment. "Or has he?"

Abigail's cheeks turned as red as the fruit in her hand. "I believe so. He. . .I saw him early this morning on the bluff."

"I see." Her mother took the topped fruits from Abigail and began cutting them into slices to go into preserves and marmalades. Others would be crushed to add to strawberry cakes and pies, while still others would be left whole and served as a dessert with fresh cream from their dairy cows. "What did he have to say about his travels?"

"Not much." Abigail shrugged and concentrated on her work. "He is very humble and credited his successes to God's abilities rather than his talents."

"He is a good man."

Abigail didn't feel like her mother's statement needed confirmation. Anyone could see Nathan Pierce was a good man. Why wouldn't he be? He was a preacher, after all. And preachers had to be good to be effective. Didn't they?

She continued pondering that question until they had all the strawberries ready to go to the kitchen. All the preachers she'd ever met were good men, some more humble than others, some more commanding behind the pulpit. But it did not necessarily follow that she should marry him—them.

She tied a cloth around her head and poured sliced strawberries into a pot on the hot stove. Mama and the cook discussed recipes and preparations, but Abigail let her thoughts wander back to her discussion with Nathan that morning.

He had been so considerate when he thought she was upset, and she had been unable to resist teasing him a little. But she would have to be careful to be more circumspect with him for two reasons. The first had to do with raising false hopes in her parents' minds. No matter what Mama said, she would like to see Abigail married with a house full of children. The second reason was that she did not want to mislead Nathan himself. She was not going to get married and try to make herself into some man's idea of the perfect spouse. The very idea was abhorrent to her.

Her mind made up, Abigail decided she would avoid Nathan Pierce. She nodded. While that might not be particularly easy to do if they were traveling by carriage, on a steamboat cruiser it ought to be a snap.

ten

"I don't think I can fit even one more item into this trunk." Abigail's mother tried to force the lid down over the stack of clothing. "Come over here and see if you can close the latches."

Abigail complied, tugging and grunting as she tried to get the leather straps cinched. "You lack at least an inch."

"Oof." Mama sat down on the lid and bounced. "How about now?"

Abigail pulled so hard on the straps that she worried they might break. "I'm sorry, but this is not going to work." She sat back on her heels. "I can probably squeeze a few things into my trunk."

"Could you?" Her mother looked at her over one shoulder. "I don't know why it takes so many outfits. Your father would chastise me for my excess if he knew what trouble I'm having with this trunk."

"That's only because he's a man. Women require more space. It's a wonder we don't need two or three trunks each. We have to have outfits for the morning and different ones for evening wear"—Abigail ticked off each category of clothing on a different finger—"walking dresses and riding habits, sleepwear and toiletries."

"Perhaps we shouldn't go to Jackson, after all. It seemed much simpler when we were going to the campground." Mama stood up, and the lid of the trunk popped back open. "Let's see what I can store in your trunk."

Soon they had the excess items neatly stowed away in Abigail's trunk.

"Are you two done?" Papa called to them from the base of

the stairs. "Nathan is here, and we're ready to load everything onto the wagon."

Abigail picked up her yellow bonnet and tied its wide white ribbon under her chin as her mother walked to the head of the stairs. She glanced in the mirror and sighed. Part of her wished to be considered beautiful, but that description had always been out of reach. She grimaced at her reflection. At least her hair was neat today, not blowing loose in the wind.

Butterflies took wing in her stomach as she considered the trip ahead. The boat ride was sure to be fun, and she was looking forward to seeing the attractions in Jackson, but what she anticipated most were the open-air church meetings. They always strengthened her faith and left her feeling rejuvenated and restored. Optimism buoyed her, and she left her bedroom with a new spring in her step.

❧

The crew did most of the work involved with loading the LeGrands' luggage onto the *Sierra Queen*, the stern-wheeler Nathan and the LeGrand family would be traveling on for the next twenty-four hours. Nathan tried to help, but he was pushed aside as the experienced men lifted the heavy trunks to their shoulders and strode to the boat. Mrs. LeGrand and her daughter would be staying in one stateroom, while he shared another with Mr. LeGrand.

Once again, Nathan marveled over their generosity. If not for their insistence, he would have had a much more arduous and lengthy trip.

"Come on, Nathan." Mr. LeGrand's voice drew his attention to the carriage. "Would you give Abigail a hand while I help my wife onto the boat?"

"Of course, sir." Nathan smiled at both of the ladies and offered an arm to the younger. "Watch your step."

Rough boards spanned the distance between the bank and the boat's deck, making a gangway for passengers. As soon as the two of them reached the center point, he could feel the wood bending slightly. Abigail's hand, which had been resting on his arm, clenched tightly. "Don't be afraid. You're safe."

"You must think me quite the ninny." Her voice was strained.

"Why would I think such a silly thing? Because you have sense enough to be cautious?" He placed his free hand over the one gripping his arm. "Once we get on the boat, you will feel differently."

She nodded and swallowed hard.

"Don't look down, Abigail. Look at me instead." He caught her gaze and held it as they crossed the rushing water. Something happened. He seemed to fall into her ebony eyes. Eyes that had gone from fear to admiration.

He felt strong enough to vanquish anything. His chest expanded, and his smile curved upward. They stepped as one onto the deck of the boat and stopped, still staring into each other's eyes. It might have been a few seconds or a few hours before he once again became aware of the activity around them.

"Thank you, Nathan." She whispered the words before pulling her hand free and walking away, the scarf on her bonnet floating back toward him as if giving him a jaunty wave. He wondered if he'd ever seen anything half so enchanting.

Somehow Nathan knew nothing would ever be the same again.

እ

"That was an excellent meal." Abigail's mother looked up at the waiter standing at her elbow.

"Thank you, ma'am." The man nodded his head as he removed her plate, piling it atop the other empty plates on the wooden tray balanced on his arm.

Papa leaned back in the mahogany chair and patted his flat

stomach. "I would be in trouble if I ate like this all the time."

Everyone at the table laughed at his pained expression.

"I agree with you, Mr. LeGrand." Nathan put his napkin on the table. "All of the courses nearly overwhelmed my senses. Soup, salad, two entrées, half-a-dozen side dishes, and fresh fruit for dessert. Perhaps we should take a stroll about the boat to stretch our legs."

"What a grand idea." Abigail sent him an approving smile and gathered her shawl. She and Mama had spent their time changing into proper attire for a formal dinner. Although their cabin was adequate, she was ready to do some exploring. She stood, bringing both men to their feet. "Please say you want to go, Mama."

"I suppose so." Her mother rolled her eyes. "But I don't plan to stay up all night traipsing about. The next few days are going to be filled with all sorts of activities, and we will all need our rest if we are going to take full advantage of them."

"I know you're right, dearest, but the sun has barely gone down." Papa held out his elbow and Mama tucked her hand under it.

"Don't blame me if you fall asleep while talking to Bishop Ross." Her smile softened the words.

Abigail felt Nathan's gaze and looked up at him. His blue eyes were warm—almost a caress. A lock of thick blond hair fell forward across his brow, and her fingers itched to reach up and smooth it back into place. She pulled at her shawl instead.

Nathan was so tall, towering over her like a veritable giant. She felt small in contrast, small and feminine. How did he manage to do that? Abigail had never felt this way before. How many other ladies had he charmed without saying even a word? Her smile slipped a notch, and she sighed. The answer would probably shock her.

He held out his arm. "Shall we join your parents?"

Still feeling the sting of her thoughts, Abigail ignored his gesture and stalked to the door. She would not be his next conquest.

When she caught up with her parents, they were talking to the captain. She joined them without a word, listening as he described the movement of the engine and how it pushed the large wheel at the end of his boat. Captain Rogers was a slender man of average height, who held himself with the stiff posture of a former military man. From the tip of his shiny bald head to the pointed toes of his gleaming boots, he was all business.

One of the crewmen scurried up and whispered something to the captain.

"Please excuse me. I must see to something." He sketched a quick bow and strode toward the wide stairs leading to the pilothouse on the topmost level of the boat.

"I hope nothing is wrong." Nathan's voice startled Abigail.

A shiver like a bead of icy springwater trickled down her spine. Why had he followed them out here? The unchristian thought shamed her immediately. Where else was Nathan going to go? Her parents had invited him along. She was the real problem. She needed to think of him as a brother. After all, as an only child she had often wished for a sibling.

"Captain Rogers has a great deal of experience on the Mississippi River." Her father answered Nathan's comment. "I'm sure he has everything under control."

One side of the hallway they were standing in was formed by the wall that housed the engine. A waist-high wooden rail formed the other side. Looking past it, she could make out the gray green foliage lining the desolate bank. "Does anyone live on the river between Natchez and Vicksburg?"

"Not many." Nathan answered her question. "But I suspect that one day soon there will be homes and businesses built out here. The river is a conduit of enterprise. It helps us move goods from one place to another."

Papa stepped to the rail. "Transportation was much more difficult before Captain Shreve removed the snags choking the river. I can remember back when steamboats first started traveling up the river. It seemed snags were sinking them almost every day. It's much safer now."

"Come along, Jeremiah." Mama tugged at his arm. "These young people don't want to hear how life was when you were their age. And I need an escort to my cabin."

"I'll come with you, Mama." Abigail took a step toward her before being waved away.

"Your father and I need to talk about a few things, honey. Why don't you young people stay out here and enjoy the river's beauty?"

"Yes, ma'am." She wondered if her mother was match-making once more. But even if she was, this was Abigail's chance to prove that she could control her attraction to the handsome pastor. She turned back to the rail where he stood.

"I don't know what I've done to offend you, Miss LeGrand."

"Nothing at all until you forgot my given name." She put both hands on the rail and squeezed hard.

"I'm sorry. . .Abigail."

Abigail nodded. Silence surrounded them, broken only by intermittent splashes from unseen wildlife. Damp air made her shiver slightly and let go of the rail to pull her shawl tighter.

"Are you cold?" His voice sounded concerned, kind.

Before she could answer, laughter erupted from the dining room they had left earlier.

He was standing so close she could feel when he twisted around to look over his shoulder. Did he wish to be elsewhere? And here she'd been attributing his thoughtful actions to romantic impulses. "It sounds like they're having a party. I'm sure you'd rather join them than attend me. I assure you I'll be fine out here. I will seek my cabin in a few minutes."

"If this boat is like others on the Mississippi, I imagine some of the passengers have begun a game of chance." He put a hand on her arm. "Abigail, please tell me what I've done to offend you so."

Her heart fluttered like a trapped bird at his touch. How could she explain her feelings when she didn't understand them herself? All she knew was that she had to erect a barrier between them or suffer grave consequences. She glanced up at him. "I. . .there's nothing wrong, Nathan. I'm. . . I've been a little preoccupied."

"What is troubling you?"

Why couldn't the man take a hint? Why must he persist in asking her questions? Perhaps if she asked him a question or two about his past she could take his attention off of her. Over the years, she had found this to be an effective stratagem. "Actually you are right. You trouble me greatly, Nathan."

His warm hand left her arm as he took a step back. He acted like she had slapped him. "Please tell me how I can rectify myself."

"Ever since you came to Natchez, I have wondered about your background." She ignored the little voice that whispered caution in her mind. "Yet each time I have tried to find out something more than the basics of where you were born and raised, you deflect my questions. I have begun to wonder if you are hiding some heinous background. Were you a bank robber? An escaped felon? Did you waylay the real Nathan Pierce and assume his identity for some nefarious purpose?"

The scrape of a floating snag distracted her for a moment. She watched the branches slide past, their brittle fingers reaching out as if to snatch at her skirt.

"Be careful, Abigail." He pulled her back from the rail. "I don't want you to be pulled overboard."

Surprised by his move, she fell back against his hard chest. He wrapped both arms around her to steady her, and for a moment she wanted to do nothing more than melt against him. All thoughts of keeping this strong man at arm's length dissipated like shadows fleeing from the rising sun. She would be foolish to deny the delicious emotions swirling through her because of his nearness.

"My past life has nothing to do with the present." His voice in her ear sent shivers running up and down her spine.

Reality collided with fantasy. The truth washed over her like the river rushing past the bow of this boat. She struggled to break his hold on her. "Let go of me."

He complied so quickly she almost fell flat on her face. As soon as she was steady, she turned to face him. "The truth must be pretty awful if you take such pains to hide it."

Sadness crossed his features, but she refused to be drawn in again. She pointed an accusing finger at his square chin. "You're a preacher, so you should be familiar with the warning of Moses in the book of Numbers: 'And be sure your sin will find you out.'"

She dropped her hand and marched away from him, fighting against looking back with every step. She was right. She knew it. But sometimes being right was a very hard thing.

eleven

Nathan rubbed at his eyes again and shook his head to clear it. He had gotten up and dressed before the sun rose to avoid waking Mr. LeGrand.

Outside, he walked from one end of the steamboat to the other. The only other people he saw were busy crewmen who were tending their duties in the boiler room, the galley, and the pilothouse. He knew the other passengers would be up and about soon, and he needed to find some tranquility before facing anyone.

If only Abigail's words had not kept rolling around in his head all night long. They had carried so much authority. *"Your sin will find you out."* He could have snatched more sleep if his conscience had allowed it. Or if he had not relived those harrowing moments again and again during the night. The struggle, the fear, the sickening feeling of the knife entering Ira Watson's body. Over and over again, he saw the man's shocked face loosen into a death mask. How could he ever ask for forgiveness? He didn't deserve it.

Because of that, he knew he did not deserve any woman's consideration, especially not a woman like Abigail LeGrand. So why had he lowered his defenses? The answer to that question was easy. He was beginning to care for her. He thought back to his feelings for Iris Landon, which were a mere shadow of what he felt for Abigail. And his attraction to Margaret had never grown past friendship. Abigail was so different—so complex and invigorating. He liked being with her, talking to her, teasing her.

How had he gone so quickly from one extreme to the

other? For a moment or two yesterday afternoon as they crossed the gangway together, he had thought she was the other part of him, the best part of him, the part God had fashioned only for him.

Maybe if he hadn't taken advantage of her misstep last night when they were alone. . .but she had felt so right in his arms. And he would have sworn she was comfortable there, too. Then she had turned into a wildcat. Her attack might not have left visible scars on him, but her words had surely cleaved his heart.

He wondered how she would act today. What would he say to her? Should he apologize? Or act as though nothing had happened last evening? If only he could turn to someone for answers. But he'd had no one since his parents' death. Uncle Richard, the man who had raised him, had never been much of a role model—a fact proven for good when the man was arrested for kidnapping.

He had friends back in Chattanooga, but no one in whom he could confide. A feeling of homesickness washed over him. But had he ever really had a home? Had God singled him out to live his life without the comforts of hearth and home? So what was this longing inside him for something more?

The sun rose over the tops of the trees, washing the eastern side of the steamboat with buttery color. Mist rose from the dark water and dissipated as sunlight warmed it. Reed-strewn banks slipped past him.

Nathan took one last turn on the deck before returning to his cabin. It was time to face whatever the coming day held.

❧

The low, mournful whistle of the steamboat called people to the water's edge as their steamboat began preparations to dock. Abigail stepped outside for her first full view of the town of Vicksburg. Even though it was bordered by the same river, this city looked very different from Natchez. Instead of featuring ramshackle saloons and ladies of ill repute, the docks here were crowded with warehouses and all sorts of businesses connected to the traffic on the river. Instead of the steep bluffs of Natchez, the bank here climbed a gentle slope to the top of the hill. Houses dotted the side of the hill, and more businesses were perched atop it.

Mama joined her at the rail and pointed. "Look, you can see a church from here."

Abigail spotted the crenellated tower and nodded. "Vicksburg looks like a growing town."

"Yes," her mother answered. "But I doubt it will ever be as busy as Natchez. Our proximity to New Orleans is part of the reason. Natchez has been around a lot longer. When I came down the river with your grandmother nearly twenty-five years ago, Vicksburg was only a bend in the river with a few homes, and Natchez was already the territorial capital."

"I remember reading about when Vicksburg finally became a town. I must have been fifteen or so." Abigail pressed a finger against her cheekbone. "I seem to remember it was named after a minister who objected to the American Revolution."

"Yes, that's right. His name was Newitt Vick. Most of his children still live here. Your aunt and uncle have visited with his daughter, Martha, at her home here. She is—"

"Here are my girls." Papa put one arm around Mama and the other around her. "Are you packed?"

Abigail stood on tiptoe and placed a kiss on his cheek. "Of course not, Papa. We were going to let you do it for us."

As they laughed at her joke, the steamboat bumped up against the dock. Immediately men began scurrying back and forth to secure it to the large wooden posts that would keep it from drifting back into the river's current.

Mama watched them for a moment. "Perhaps we should

go into the dining room to wait until it's time to disembark."

"Good idea." Papa strode to the entrance and held the door open for them to enter.

They sat at the nearest empty table and watched through the wide windows as the crewmen secured the boat. Abigail would have liked to watch them more closely, but she knew it was better to stay out of the way. A waiter came over to their table and asked if they would care for refreshments. Abigail shook her head. She was much too excited to be able to eat or drink.

After he dismissed the waiter, Papa turned back to her. "Have you seen our preacher this morning, Abigail?"

Her excitement ebbed. "No, sir." She frowned at him. "Is he not still in your cabin?"

"He was gone before I awoke this morning." Papa leaned back in his chair and crossed his legs at the ankles. "I was concerned that he may have jumped overboard after your walk last night."

Abigail spluttered. "I. . .I don't know what you mean."

Her mother raised an eyebrow as she glanced toward her daughter. "Although I don't remember your looking particularly guilty last night, I also cannot remember you giving me a reason for your early return to our cabin."

"I'm afraid I am the reason for her discomfort." Nathan's voice startled Abigail.

When had he come into the room? Why hadn't she kept a better eye on the door? Why had the room grown so small? Hot blood burned her neck and cheeks. She could feel all their gazes on her. She wished she could simply melt into the wooden planks at her feet and float away in the water beneath the boat.

"It was nothing." She cleared her throat. "I. . .a tree. . .um. . . a tree scraped against the boat and I almost fell. . .and Na— Brother Pierce pulled me away from the edge."

"I see." Her mother's voice brimmed with mirth.

Her father uncrossed his ankles and stood. "I owe you my thanks, sir. I appreciate your saving my daughter."

"It was nothing." Nathan took the hand her father offered. "I only regret upsetting her." He turned those deep blue eyes to Abigail. This morning they reminded her of a favorite velvet dress she'd worn when she was younger. "Please accept my apologies, Miss LeGrand."

What? He was apologizing to her? Abigail closed her mouth with an audible snap when she realized it was hanging open. The accusations she had flung at him last night came back to her with sterling clarity. "I'm afraid I acted much worse than you, sir."

A choked sound to her right was likely her mama trying to hide her laughter. Abigail's embarrassment deepened.

Nathan bowed to her. "Let's put the whole incident behind us."

"Well said, Brother Pierce." Her father was beaming at the man.

Abigail wanted to stomp her foot. Papa, too? Was her whole family turning against her? It seemed Nathan had won both their hearts. But losing her temper would do nothing to advance her case, so she pinned a smile on her face and nodded agreement.

She would show him. She would be so kind to Brother Pierce it would be like heaping coals of shame on his head. Then he would show his true colors and maybe her parents would realize he wasn't the perfect man they imagined him to be.

❧

Bridgeport Road, the stagecoach route between Vicksburg and Jackson, was a narrow lane with a surfeit of potholes and ruts. Abigail clasped her hands on her lap and tried to keep from touching the passengers on either side of her. She should have known this was a bad idea when she first caught sight of the driver.

His face was dark from a combination of sun and dirt. Even though it was quite warm, he wore a faded knit cap on his grizzled hair. His clothing was rumpled and faded, and his manner was gruff. He did not help her or her mother climb into his coach.

She glanced toward Nathan out of the corner of her eye. He was lucky enough to be sitting next to the window and seemed enthralled by the countryside they were passing through. His shoulders blocked most of her view, although she could see the tops of large pine trees and an occasional horseman.

"Mississippi is so different from Tennessee. No mountains. No waterfalls. Only an endless sea of trees." Nathan turned his serious blue gaze on her.

Would she be overstepping his boundaries by asking about his home? He was so secretive about his past. Yet his comment seemed like an invitation.

Before Abigail could formulate a question that would not seem like it was prying into his past, her mother spoke up from her position on the opposite seat. "I lived for a while in Nashville, but I understand it is nothing like Chattanooga."

"When I was a young boy, many of those living in the area were Cherokee. Ross's Landing, across the river from us, was the first outpost and was built by John Ross, the chief of the Cherokee."

Papa frowned at his words. "I thought you lived in Chattanooga."

"Yes, sir, but we didn't call it that until a few years ago. In fact, my store is actually located in Daisy. It's right close to Chattanooga. If Chattanooga keeps on growing like it has in the past few years, it'll probably swallow Daisy whole."

No one said anything for a few minutes. The stagecoach

hit a rut and lurched. Abigail held herself as well as she could manage. Nathan swayed with the motion of the conveyance and their shoulders rubbed together for a few moments. The contact set off a covey of birds in her stomach. She jerked away from him, bumping into the poor woman on her left.

Nathan glanced toward her, then away. He cleared his throat and spoke to her parents. "I don't know exactly what to expect when we get to Jackson."

"I don't either, Papa. Will it be like when we go to Gatlin's Camp Ground later this month?"

"No." Papa shook his head. "This is going to be a meeting of the church leaders, the men who will decide the appropriate path for our denomination over the next year."

Her mother hid a yawn behind her hand. "We probably won't even be part of the meeting, Abigail. We'll be expected to help everything go smoothly, from the meals to the care of the children."

That was not fair. She'd much rather attend the meeting than be stuck washing dishes and changing diapers.

Conversation dwindled as the interior of the coach warmed under the June sun. Mama dozed, her head on Papa's shoulder. He had pulled out a small book and was reading it with great concentration. Abigail was able to watch the scenery since Nathan had shifted his position. Dense forests eventually gave way to sparsely populated areas. She saw a man working to fell a tree next to a log cabin. A garden farther down the road was being worked by a woman in a straw bonnet, her children at her side.

Then the houses grew closer together, signaling that they were nearing town. She could hear dogs barking as they chased the stagecoach. The vehicle came to a stop at a busy corner. Abigail could barely contain her excitement.

Her mother sat up and blinked rapidly. "Have we arrived?"

"Yes, dear." Papa smiled gently down at her.

Abigail could not help the warm feeling in her chest. It was so wonderful to see the love her parents still held for each other. She knew it was founded on their mutual love for God and Christ, faith that kept them strong in the face of adversity and kept them stable during times of prosperity. She wondered if she would ever feel the same for any man.

Nathan swung open the door and jumped down. Then he turned and offered his hand to Abigail. She hesitated a moment before putting her hand in his. What if the same combustible reaction occurred? Not wanting to take the chance, she gathered her skirts and stood up, bending over slightly because of the low ceiling. She was very aware of the gazes of the other passengers as she began her descent.

Abigail almost made it to the ground when one of the dogs came running up, barking loudly. Startled, she lost her balance with one foot on the mounting block. She dropped her skirts and windmilled her arms to keep herself from falling. Her heart stuttered as she realized she would not be able to stop her headlong plunge. A muscular arm snaked around her waist before she hit the ground. Abigail was once again pulled up to Nathan's chest, but today she was facing him. Her nose rubbed against one of the buttons on his coat, and she breathed in the fresh, manly scent of him.

"Are you okay?" His voice was deep, with a gruff edge. As though he'd been frightened, too.

Her father exited the coach quickly. "Are you all right, Abigail?"

No was the answer she wanted to give to both of them. Her pride was in tatters, and her heart was beating so quickly she thought it might burst through her bodice. She pushed against Nathan's hard chest, relieved to find she could stand on her own two feet. "Yes, thank you both for your concern."

The stagecoach had stopped in front of an inn, but she had no idea if it was the place they were staying or not. It was big—five-stories high—and busy. The grounds around them looked more like a market than anything else. Pigs rooted in one corner while chickens scooted between the booted feet of the stablemen.

Abigail felt somewhat overwhelmed by the noise, smells, and activity surging around her. Perhaps she should not have been in such a rush to leave the protection of Nathan's arms. An arresting thought struck her. Was God showing her that independence had its drawbacks?

twelve

"It's about time for you to wake up, daughter." Mama's voice interrupted her dream.

Abigail groaned and rolled over, trying to pull the quilt up over her eyes. "Please don't tell me it's already morning."

"Yes." Mama whipped the quilt away. She must have already pulled back the draperies from the room's east-facing window because sunlight flooded the room. "If we don't hurry, your papa will be finished with his breakfast before we get downstairs."

Another groan slipped from Abigail's lips as she sat up. "I feel like someone whipped me during the night."

Mama put a cool hand on her forehead. "Are you sick?"

Yellow fever was a constant fear, especially in the spring and summer months. "No, ma'am. I'm only sore from all the bouncing of that stagecoach."

She could see the relief in her mother's expression and determined not to complain further about her minor aches and pains. They would fade anyway, once she was up and about. Taking her wrapper from the foot of the bed, she cleaned her face and hands with water from the inn's pitcher while her mother pulled out Abigail's plainest dress of drab brown homespun. "Are we going to be cleaning today?"

Mama nodded as she shook out the skirts. "And cooking." She glanced down at her own gray homespun. "At least that is what your papa says."

Abigail almost protested. She would much rather join the gentlemen in their meetings. But she knew it was impossible. Her parents were lenient with her at home, but here they would wish for her to be circumspect.

As soon as Abigail was dressed and her hair had been pulled into a neat bun at the base of her neck, the two women went downstairs to the dining room. Nathan and Papa were drinking coffee and talking quietly as they entered.

Nathan saw them first and came to his feet. "Good morning, ladies. I trust you slept well."

Her father also stood and beckoned them to the table as they exchanged greetings. As soon as they were seated, a servant brought several bowls of food—eggs, sausage, biscuits, and grits—to be passed among the diners.

She noticed an odd expression on Nathan's face as he accepted the bowl of grits from her father. "Have you never eaten grits before?"

Nathan shook his head. "What are they?"

"They're grits. Do you mean to tell me you don't have any grit trees in Tennessee?" She bit the inside of her cheek to keep from laughing at the look on his face.

"No, I don't think so." His voice was hesitant. "What do they look like?"

"In the springtime, when they flower, the trees are covered with lots of grits. People put out baskets and wait for all the grits to fall into them. Of course, sometimes their children climb into the trees and shake the limbs to get the grits to fall off faster. You probably saw some of them on your way to Mississippi."

The look on his face was priceless. Nathan had no idea whether to believe her or not. He glanced toward her parents, who were studiously avoiding his gaze. Abigail put a hand to her mouth to hold in the laughter, but a giggle escaped. That was enough to set off her parents' laughter.

She put her hand down, and her laughter joined theirs. At first she wasn't sure if the pastor was going to take offense at being the target of her teasing. Then his lips turned up, and soon he was laughing with them. It was exactly what was needed to ease the tension between all of them.

Mama finally took pity on the pastor and explained that grits were nothing more than ground corn. He piled some on his plate and added butter at her urging.

The talk turned general, and Abigail delved into a newspaper article that caught her attention. She nibbled at a biscuit and shook her head over the story about a slave uprising in Alabama.

"What has brought such a dark frown to you on this lovely morning?" The question came from Nathan.

She shrugged her shoulders and folded the paper. "I don't know why our fellow Southerners cling so firmly to slavery."

Her father nodded. "That's an issue that is bound to come up this weekend. Our church leaders need to speak out more openly in favor of abolition. It would help so many to see the truth."

As her mother expressed her approval of Papa's statement, Abigail glanced at Nathan. Would he speak his own beliefs or keep them to himself? A part of her wished he would express his ideas in front of her parents for two reasons: They would no longer think him such a perfect paragon of virtue and intelligence, and they would immediately begin to try to show him the error of his thinking.

But he remained silent, listening as her papa talked about the importance of treating every person with Christian kindness and how easy it was to make a living even without using slave labor. She had heard his speech many times in the past but hoped some of his points would sink into Nathan's mind and begin to work a change.

"I know how it is to believe slavery is not evil." Her mother's words got her attention. This was something she'd not heard before. "My parents owned slaves even before I was born, so I thought nothing of the matter." She reached out for her husband's hand. "But once I met you, I learned the error of my ways. I began to see Jemma and the others as people with talents as important as mine."

Papa shook his head. "It was your faith that led you to the truth."

"Perhaps so, but I seem to remember a fiery young man who was determined to rebel against everyone to prove his beliefs."

Their love was so touching to see. Abigail glanced toward Nathan and wondered what was going through his mind. Was he embarrassed by her parents' obvious affection for each other? Defensiveness filled her. If he dared to even hint at disdain, she would give him a tongue-lashing he'd not soon forget.

Nathan looked away from her parents and met her gaze. For a moment it was as if she could see past the bright blue of his eyes and into his very soul. The longing she saw there made her want to reach out to him. She wanted to hold him close and reassure him that God loved him no matter what. But as quickly as it had appeared, the pain vanished, replaced by his usual calm expression. Had she only imagined the emotion in his gaze, or had it been real?

Abigail's unkind thoughts melted away, replaced by sympathy. What kind of life had this man experienced before coming to Mississippi? Was the profound grief she thought she had seen a few seconds earlier the reason he didn't want to talk about the past? And more importantly, what kind of future did he anticipate for himself?

❧

"Abigail, would you melt some butter in that pan on the stove?" Mrs. Gail Ross, the wife of Bishop Bill Ross, handed her some freshly churned butter before turning back to supervise two young girls who were layering peaches into a cast-iron dutch oven. "That's right, Gabrielle, add some sugar now, and we'll see about rolling out a crust."

The kitchen was a hive of activity as the women worked to feed the church elders who would soon be through with their meeting. Wonderful aromas of fried chicken, stew, and collard greens filled the warm room.

Abigail dropped the butter into the hot pan and stirred it with a spoon. "What am I making?"

Her mother walked over and stirred a pot of collard greens that had been picked earlier that morning. "Creamed corn." Mama's answer made Abigail's mouth water.

She had already helped to make several skillets of cornbread from locally milled grain, and she had peeled enough potatoes to feed an entire army. At first it had been fun to compete with the other young women to see who could produce the longest and thinnest peel, but after the first hour, even that did not distract anyone from the tedium of their task. Once they had peeled every potato, they took them outside and placed them in a huge cauldron of water boiling over an open fire.

Mrs. Ross brought a bowl of brown sugar to the stove and leaned over Abigail's shoulder. "What a good job you're doing. Now take this and stir it in slowly." She walked to the door and called out to the children sitting on the back porch. "Are y'all done shelling that corn yet? We're going to need it right soon."

Abigail was amazed at the energy that kept Mrs. Ross moving from station to station. She was a small woman—about an inch shorter than Abigail—but what she lacked in height, she made up for in enthusiasm and zeal.

As soon as they had arrived a couple of hours earlier, Abigail and her mother had been given aprons and separated from the menfolk. Mrs. Ross and Mama had discussed the menu for a midafternoon feast before parceling out tasks to all the people in the kitchen. It was a good thing Bishop and Mrs. Ross had four children or not everything would have been ready in time.

"Here's the corn." Mrs. Ross brought a large bowl of bright yellow kernels to Abigail and set them down on the counter at her left elbow. "You'll have to keep stirring until the corn is done. Gertrude, go get the cream for Miss LeGrand's corn." Then she was off again, checking one dish or another, waving flies away, and marshaling the younger children to wash dishes while the others continued cooking.

Eventually everything was ready, from the first course—leek soup—to the dessert—deep-dish peach cobbler. The dining-room table had been set, and all they needed was for the men to appear.

Abigail blew out a tired sigh as she pulled off her apron. "I don't think I ever appreciated how much work it takes to feed a large group of people." She plopped down in an empty chair. One of the twin girls—she wasn't sure if it was Gabrielle or Gertrude—handed her a cup of water from the well outside. Its cool moisture was a relief to her parched throat.

"Yes, we so seldom have more than a few people come by for dinner." Her mother sat down beside her at the kitchen table. Abigail tried to hand her the half-empty cup in her hand, but the other twin appeared with a fresh cup. "Thank you, Gabrielle."

Now, how did Mama tell them apart? She glanced at the two girls who wore their aprons like badges of honor. From the braids of their red-blond hair to the tips of their brown leather shoes, they looked identical to her eyes.

"I appreciate all the hard work you ladies did this morning." Mrs. Ross darted back inside after overseeing the dishwashers on the back porch. "It's a delight to have so many willing workers." She smiled at the twins and held out her arms for a hug. "And I cannot wait until we see your father's face when he tries a bite of that peach cobbler."

They giggled as they kissed their mother's cheeks, one on

either side. One more hug, and she sent them upstairs to their bedrooms to clean up before the meal, leaving the three older women alone for a minute.

"I wonder why the meeting is taking so long." Mrs. Ross glanced around the kitchen. "They are generally finished by two o'clock."

Her mother shook her head. "We live in chaotic times. I am afraid the issue of slavery is causing a rift in the church."

"How can Christian people truly support such a terrible institution?" Abigail pushed herself up from the table and walked to a large window overlooking several leafy oak trees. Flowers waved gaily under their shade.

"It's not our place to judge them." Mrs. Ross's voice was gentle. "But we have the duty to pray for them."

Her mother laughed. "You sound like Jeremiah. My husband is determined to teach by example and pray for God's intervention. Even during those early days when he was the victim of an evil plot, he refused to do anything more than make certain their plans did not hurt me or his workers."

Abigail listened to the two women discussing the issues, amazed that neither of them felt they should try to change their husbands' minds. She turned to them. "How do you do it? How do you sit back and discuss this without trying to make a difference?"

Mrs. Ross looked confused by the question. "Are you talking about trying to undermine our husbands' decisions?"

Before Abigail could answer, her mother spoke up. "Abigail, we have spoken about this before. The Bible teaches us to submit to our husbands. They are the heads of our households."

"That's right." Mrs. Ross twisted her wedding ring as she hesitated. "My husband and I each have our duties to fulfill. If I tried to usurp his work, or he mine, our family could not function. Bill helps people turn their lives and hearts to Jesus, while my ministry has more to do with their earthly needs."

When Mrs. Ross explained it that way, it made more sense to Abigail. She had seen the same in her own household while growing up, but she had chafed against the restrictions she thought constrained her mother. Had she been that mistaken? "What about suffrage for women?"

Mrs. Ross shrugged. "Mississippi was the first state to recognize the rights of married women to own property separate from their husbands. How much more progressive would you have us be?"

"I would like to be a part of this state's future." Abigail clenched her fist. She had been raised by parents who believed strongly in abolishing slavery. She believed allowing women to vote was almost as important. "I do not want to be treated as though I have no brain for anything beyond housekeeping, motherhood, and clothing fashions."

"Are you saying you think those pursuits have no validity?" Her mother's tones held a note of amusement.

Feeling as though she had been betrayed, Abigail turned to look at her mother. "Of course not. I would not be so foolish. Many women don't aspire to more than keeping an immaculate home and raising their children, but others would like to do something different. Women like Lucretia Mott and Margaret Fuller."

Abigail watched as the two older women exchanged glances. Volumes of information and experience seemed to pass between them. As though they knew something more than she.

Abigail sat back down at the table. Forcing herself to relax, she took a deep, calming breath, and placed her hands in her lap.

Mrs. Ross leaned over and gave her shoulder a pat. "You will understand better once you fall in love. Then you will see the importance of supporting your husband's decisions. Paul's words are not to be ignored lightly. If wives were to try and rule over their husbands, this world would soon be a place of much bitterness and rivalry. Besides, I am sure you will find as much satisfaction in submitting to your husband as I do. When a man truly loves you as Christ loves the Church, you will have no trouble doing so."

Struggling for a moment with the conflicting thoughts in her head, Abigail glanced at her mother and heeded the warning she saw. As someone younger than their hostess as well as an unmarried female, she knew she could not continue to argue the point. Dropping her gaze to her hands, she nodded. "I hope you're right."

"Of course she is." Mama looked relieved. She might have added something more to the conversation, but the sound of male voices in the dining room forestalled her. She stood and held out a hand to Abigail. "Let's go find out what happened in the meeting."

Even though she had great interest in that very thing, Abigail wished she had time to sit quietly and think about what the two women had told her. Was there validity in Paul's instructions to women? Was there an order to things that must be preserved? She did not know the answer, only that she still wanted to plan her own path without having to please some man's arbitrary whim.

thirteen

After the Sunday service and a lively meal with the Ross family, Nathan returned to the inn with the LeGrands. The past two days had been filled with so much information he wondered his head did not explode.

Leaning back against the meager cushions of the rented carriage, he pondered what to do for the afternoon. He wasn't tired, so the idea of an afternoon nap did not appeal. Should he closet himself in his rooms and study his Bible? Perhaps, but this was his first visit to Mississippi's capital city, so he should be able to find an interesting way to spend the rest of the day.

Mrs. LeGrand's voice interrupted his musings. "What do you plan to do this afternoon?"

Nathan raised his head and looked toward her, wondering if she had read his mind. But she was looking toward her daughter, not at him.

Abigail shrugged. "I don't know."

"I have an idea." Mr. LeGrand winked at his daughter. "Why don't you and Brother Pierce explore the city? You could tour the State House. I understand it is quite spectacular in its scope. And Pastor Ross told me the governor's home is nearly complete."

Abigail shook her head. "I don't think—"

"What a wonderful idea!" Her mother's exclamation cut off Abigail's refusal. "The two of you can come back this afternoon and tell us all about it."

"I would not mind seeing the State House." Was that his voice? Had he lost his mind? It was obvious Abigail had no interest in touring with him. He should have demurred. So why was he nodding?

"Good." Mr. LeGrand cleared his throat. "That's settled then. We will let you young people ramble about while we make arrangements for the trip home."

For her part, Abigail said nothing more. But she did not look at him a single time during the rest of the ride to the inn.

Nathan had the idea she was not going to make the best traveling companion, but he did not mind trying to cajole her a little. He would like to return to the easy camaraderie they had shared prior to the steamboat voyage. He liked Abigail very much, possibly a little too much, and he chafed against the polite wall she had erected between them. Perhaps this would give them the opportunity to clear the air between them.

⁂

"Right this way, ma'am, sir." A tall, smiling man wearing a fancy coat and tall cravat led the way to the second floor of the State House. "It's so nice to see a young married couple taking an interest in the seat of government."

Abigail's cheeks burned. "But we're not married."

She was surprised at the grin on Nathan's face, which made her cheeks heat up another one hundred degrees or so. What did he find so funny?

"My apologies." The man glanced at both of them. "I guess it's the way the two of you look together, kind of natural like."

What should she make of that comment? After hesitating for a moment, she decided the best way to deal with the situation was to pretend deafness. Nathan proffered his arm but she shook her head slightly. No sense in strengthening their guide's supposition.

Stepping into the main atrium, she was nearly overwhelmed

by the size and appointments of the State House. It was definitely a fitting place for decision makers to meet.

Their guide pointed out the gleaming limestone floors and had them look upward some ninety-four feet at the dome above the rotunda. As he led them up a sweeping staircase, he talked about the first, failed architect, John Lawrence, who had been fired when he botched the contracted work for three straight years. His voice warmed considerably as he spoke of William Nichols, the final architect who tore out his predecessor's work and started over in 1835.

They reached the second floor and followed him to the rail that surrounded a large opening overlooking the entry foyer. "As I'm sure you are aware, Mississippi has a bicameral legislature. When they are meeting, the Senate occupies the room to our left, while the House meets in the room to our right."

Abigail looked at the wide doors on either end of the hallway. "You can see from one side all the way to the other."

"What a perceptive young lady you are escorting, sir."

"She is indeed." Nathan's blue gaze swept her face.

The knowing look on the guide's face made Abigail fold her lips in a tight line. He glanced at her and cleared his throat. "Well. . .as I was saying. . .or rather, as you pointed out, miss, the chamber doors allow the presiding officers to see each other. That way the lieutenant governor and the Speaker of the House can begin and end their sessions simultaneously."

"Does the governor have an office in the State House?" Nathan nodded toward the closed doors lined up with military precision along the hallway between the two chambers.

"Yes, he does. And if we're lucky, you may see Governor McNutt during your visit here. His office is on this floor, to one side of the Supreme Court Chamber directly behind us."

"So all three branches of government are housed in this one building?" Abigail felt her mouth drop open. The building seemed so quiet, yet it must be a beehive of activity at some times of the year.

The guide recaptured her attention. "Let's go up one floor, and I'll show you the galleries where the public can watch the proceedings of the legislature."

"Even ladies?" The question popped out of her mouth before she could stop it.

The guide smiled. "Of course. We in Mississippi revere our women. We would never try to exclude them."

Except from voting or holding office. At least those words stayed inside her mind instead of tripping off her tongue. She had no desire to offend the tour guide, even though he hadn't been very considerate of her feelings. It wasn't his fault women had not been granted suffrage.

They sat in the wooden chairs in the gallery, and she closed her eyes to imagine what the chamber below her must be like while the legislature was meeting. Serious discussions, motions, bills, resolutions. She had read about the legislators' work in the newspaper, but it was so exciting to actually be here. To see the place where they debated and discussed and crafted the laws of the land made her blood pump faster. Perhaps one day she could talk Papa into bringing her back when the legislature was in session.

"Abigail?" Nathan's voice penetrated her thoughts. "Are you ready to go?"

The visions faded along with her excitement. How long had she been daydreaming? Nathan was still sitting next to her, but the guide had returned to the door and was looking at his pocket watch.

"I suppose it's time for us to leave." She picked up her reticule and stood.

The guide put his watch back into the pocket of his waistcoat and led them back down the stairs to the first floor. She and Nathan followed his footsteps like a couple of baby ducklings trailing behind their mama. At the entrance, the guide handed Nathan his hat. "Are the two of you going to see the new governor's home?"

"I had understood it's not complete."

"Almost." The man pointed toward the south. "Visitors are welcome even though many rooms are not furnished. It's election year, you know. I suppose the new governor and first lady will bring their own things with them."

"Thank you for directing us." Nathan pulled a coin from his pocket and offered it to the guide.

"Thank you, sir." He pocketed the coin without glancing at it. "You can take a carriage if necessary, but the mansion is three blocks down Capitol Street."

Abigail felt a bit put out. Why were the two men talking as if she didn't exist? Did her opinion not matter? What if her feet hurt after traipsing all over the State House? Or what if she had no desire to see the mansion? Nathan couldn't know how keen she was to see it. She might have had plans to do something completely different back at the hotel, but did that occur to Nathan? No. He simply held out his arm as if he expected her to fall in with whatever plan he devised. She would not stand for such treatment. "I don't believe I can walk another step."

His head swiveled toward her and his blue eyes narrowed. Was he about to order her to accompany him?

Her chin tilted upward. She would not be cowed by any man.

"What's wrong, Abigail?"

Shame washed through her at the concern in his voice. A sharp thought, however, overrode it. It was about time he considered her opinion. It didn't really matter that she was not overtired. The point was his lack of consideration. His attempt to control her. "I am a bit weary, but please don't let me stop your sightseeing. You go on to the mansion. I'm certain I can manage to find my way back to the hotel."

A frown darkened his brow, turning the sky blue color of his eyes stormy gray. Her chin went up and her spine straightened. She was a grown woman and could take care of herself. She would not cower before any man.

He took her hand and drew her a few steps away from the interested ears of their guide. "I am sorry, but I cannot allow you to do that."

She could feel her eyes narrowing at his statement. "You cannot allow it? I'll have you know I am perfectly capable of managing my own life." She jerked her hand away and turned to descend the steps. If she had to walk every step of the way back to the hotel she would do it.

"Abigail, wait. I'll gladly escort you to your parents if that's your wish. But you should not wander the streets alone. I'm sure pickpockets and thieves abound in such a populous area."

She could hear his footsteps behind her but refused to turn her head. Thank goodness the carriage that had brought them to the State House was still there. She marched straight to it and smiled at the driver as he opened the door for her. She had barely sat down, however, before *he* climbed into the carriage and took the opposite seat.

"I don't know what I've said to set you off this time, Miss LeGrand, but whatever it is, I pray you will explain it to me so I can apologize and we can go on as before."

She raised her chin and looked him straight in the eye. "I have no idea what you mean, Mr. Pierce. It is a pity you do not trust me to take care of myself, but since that is the case, I suppose you shall reap the consequences." Feeling she had put him in his place without uttering a single cross word, Abigail congratulated herself. She turned to gaze at the scenery outside and completely ignored the clamoring voice of her conscience as the carriage retraced the route to their inn.

fourteen

Nathan prepared to make the rounds of his circuit once again. Although he would rather have rested a day or two after returning from Jackson, it was probably a good idea for him to maintain a discreet distance between himself and his host's daughter. But before he could go, he would have to take his leave of her. . .them.

Nathan put on his best frock coat and hat and strode to the main house. He knew Mrs. LeGrand entertained guests at this time of the morning. Perhaps her daughter would be out on errands, and he wouldn't even have to see her. That would be best for both of them. He noticed two carriages at the front door, a sure sign of several visitors. So even if Abigail was here, she would likely be preoccupied by other conversations.

Taking the front steps two at a time, he grabbed the brass door knocker and rapped it smartly against the LeGrands' front door.

The housekeeper opened the door and wiped her hands on her checkered apron. "Good mornin', Mr. Pierce." The black woman's drawl was as thick and sweet as honey. "Come on in here. The missus is in the parlor."

The hope that *she* might not be in the parlor died as he heard Abigail's lilting laughter. He took a deep breath before walking into the room. Mrs. LeGrand and her daughter shared the sofa, each talking to a different visitor. Mrs. LeGrand left off talking to her friend Mrs. Hughes and greeted him, but Abigail smiled briefly before returning her attention to Silas Ward, the man sitting in a chair next to her end of the sofa.

A sick feeling invaded his stomach at the sight of the man's hand brushing her arm as he put down his china cup. No one else seemed to notice the familiar way he was acting, so Nathan averted his gaze and tried to concentrate on Mrs. LeGrand.

"Why don't you sit here, Nathan?" She indicated a spot on the sofa. If he took it, he would be sitting between her and her daughter. "I was telling Susannah about our trip to Jackson. Perhaps you can tell her about the meeting with the church elders."

Nathan eased onto the sofa, careful to avoid touching Abigail. Mrs. LeGrand poured tea into a delicate china cup, added a sugar cube at his nod, and stirred it delicately before handing it to him. "We talked about abolition mostly."

Susannah sipped from her teacup and nodded. "I assume some of our local pastors do not like the church's support of abolition."

"That's right." He wondered if Abigail was listening to their conversation. "I have to admit I didn't understand much about the whole issue of slavery until I came to Mississippi."

"In the part of Tennessee where Nathan lived, they don't have many slaves." Mrs. LeGrand touched his hand lightly. "But we've been praying for his eyes to be opened to the true evil of owning another person, isn't that right, Abigail?"

"What?" The girl sitting on his other side looked past him toward her mother. "I'm afraid I wasn't paying attention. Mr. Ward has been telling me about his latest visit to the orphanage."

Mrs. LeGrand repeated her statement.

Abigail shrugged. "Anyone with half a brain could see for himself. I'm sure you don't support the institution of slavery, do you, Mr. Ward?"

The man shivered. "No. My uncle and I hired help over the years, but I cannot imagine purchasing another person."

"Where did you grow up, Mr. Ward?" Susannah Hughes asked the question.

His gaze shifted to the floor before he spoke. Nathan wondered if he was marshaling his thoughts or coming up with a falsehood to share with the group. Then he berated himself. Why did he dislike the man so much? Was it because of Mr. Ward's obvious interest in Abigail? Or because she seemed open to his interest?

"To tell the truth, ma'am, we lived all over. My uncle was a bit of a wanderer."

"You poor thing." Abigail leaned forward and put her hand over his. "That's no kind of life for a child."

"No, no. I was lucky to have someone to care for me. Not like the poor orphans back in town who have no family to claim them."

Nathan wanted to roll his eyes at the man's obviously calculated response. But all of the women in the room were nodding. Was he the only one who could see the truth? In that moment he made a decision. He would stay around a day or two and make certain Mr. Ward was not making himself a nuisance in the LeGrand home. Perhaps he would even do some checking and try to find out exactly why the man had come to Natchez.

"Your concern is praiseworthy." Nathan tried to make his tone admiring. At least his statement earned a kind glance from Abigail. But the words stuck in his throat like a clump of mud.

Mrs. LeGrand offered him a lemon cookie from the serving tray. "That reminds me, Nathan, before you came in, Abigail was discussing having a picnic for the orphans. I'm sure you would like to join her."

Nathan started to shake his head. The very thought of having to spend an extended amount of time surrounded by children made him shiver like a fall leaf. Maybe he shouldn't postpone his plans after all. He could always investigate the mysterious Mr. Ward when he returned.

Before he could form the polite refusal, however, Abigail spoke up. "Mama, I'm sure Brother Pierce is much too busy to waste his time with such a frivolous activity."

"Yes, I doubt he would enjoy sitting on the ground with a bunch of children." Mr. Ward tittered. "I'm sure he'd find it far beneath the dignity of a pastor."

"Not at all. I would love to come." Nathan took a bite out of the lemon cookie as silence invaded the room. As its sweetness melted on his tongue, he wondered if he had completely lost his senses.

❧

"I love you."

The look on Brother Pierce's face was priceless. It reminded Abigail of the time a snake had spooked her horse—the wild-eyed gaze, the way his head swiveled around. She almost expected to see him jump up from the blanket and take off for the woods. Should she intervene? Or let Mia continue to terrorize the man? She decided on the former. "Mia, I need some help washing our dishes in the stream."

The six-year-old sighed. "I wish we could talk some more, Preacher."

Abigail clapped her hands to get the girl's attention. "Mia."

"Yes, ma'am." She got up off the blanket they had used for a table and meandered toward the baskets full of dirty dishes and leftover food where Abigail stood.

"Take these cups to the edge of the water. See the towel I set out to dry them on? We'll be on the strip of sand right next to it. I'll be right behind you with the plates and saucers."

As they passed the blanket, Nathan sent her a thankful glance. She hid her grin. Why had the man decided to come when it was so obvious he did not know how to interact with children? All morning he had been stiff and non-talkative with all but the oldest boys. But she had to admit he'd been good with them, talking about male-oriented topics—hunting, fishing, and horses. With that group, he had been much more popular than poor Mr. Ward, who seemed to know nothing about horseflesh, shooting, or choosing bait.

"Don't you think he's the most handsome man you've ever met?" Mia's blue eyes, so similar in color to Nathan's, had a dreamy quality.

Abigail hid her smile. "I can see you think so. But you should be spending more time playing with the others instead of bothering Brother Pierce."

Mia rinsed out a cup and placed it on the towel Abigail had brought to the stream earlier. "I wish he would 'dopt me."

Settling next to the girl on the sandy bank, Abigail wondered how best to handle the situation. Her heart ached at the poignancy in Mia's voice. Sometimes it was hard not to bring all of them home to live with her and her parents. "You have to remember Brother Pierce is not married. He would not be able to take care of a little girl, especially since he has to travel to other churches so often."

The sounds of the nearby woods enveloped them as the two rinsed the dirty dishes, but it didn't seem to matter to Mia. Her shoulders drooped, and she ran her sleeve across her face. Then Mia's head popped up and her wide eyes searched Abigail's face. "I know what to do. You can marry him! And then the two of you could 'dopt me, and we could make a happy family. I would work really hard every day, and you wouldn't have to do anything 'cept eat cookies and pies."

Abigail's mouth dropped open. She glanced back over her shoulder to see if anyone had heard Mia's outrageous suggestion. She had no doubt she would die of embarrassment if Nathan was listening. But he seemed to be engrossed in the core of an apple he held in his hand. She breathed a prayer of thankfulness and turned to the precocious young girl. "That is out of the question, I'm afraid. I am determined to remain unmarried so I can control my future. When you get a little older, you will begin to understand."

Mia's shoulders sagged once more. She looked down into the clear water. "I guess then"—her voice caught—"I'll have to find another lady to marry him."

The way Abigail's stomach churned at Mia's words, one would think she cared whether or not Nathan married someone else. And she certainly did not care. Not at all.

&

"You must play blindman's bluff with us, Miss LeGrand." The plea on Silas's face was impossible to resist. They had put away all the food and would soon have to load everyone into the wagon to head back to the orphanage. But she supposed they could play one more game.

The children added their voices to his request. Abigail removed her bonnet and stood, glancing at the blanket where Nathan lounged. "Come along, Brother Pierce. We cannot disappoint the children."

He shook his head. "I am content to watch, and I think you might want to reconsider it yourself now that the day has grown so warm. You are bound to get hot and dirty."

Unaccommodating, overbearing man. How dare he try to dictate what she should do? He could stay in the shade if he wanted to. She would not sit here while the rest of them enjoyed the game. She put her nose up to show her disdain and turned to Silas. "I'll play as long as I don't have to wear the blindfold first."

"Agreed." Silas picked up an unused napkin and rolled it into a serviceable blindfold. "I'll be first." He tied the napkin around his head and held out his hands. "Now where can I find someone to take my place?"

The children scattered about the open area, giggling and

whispering to each other as he wandered about with his hands in front of him. His questing fingers finally found one of the older girls, and he pulled off the napkin. "Now it's your turn."

She was in turn teased and taunted by the other players until she grabbed hold of another child's collar. Abigail moved about quickly to avoid capture when she realized that Nathan was no longer sitting on the blanket. Where had he gone? She could not see him at the wagon. Had he wandered off into the woods and gotten lost? Swampy areas in the woods were filled with snakes, poisonous spiders, and even an alligator or two. Distracted by her concern, she failed to notice the blindfolded player near her. When his sticky fingers grabbed her sleeve, she groaned.

The little boy, Evan Jumper, pulled off the blindfold and handed it to her. She started to tie it around her hair when someone's hands came from behind her and took away the piece of linen cloth. She glanced over her shoulder. "Silas."

"Please let me."

Abigail smiled, wishing the preacher was here so he could hear her next comment. "You're such a gentleman, Mr. Ward."

"It's the least I can do since I'm the one who got you involved in the first place."

Abigail raised her eyebrows. "That's right, you did."

"Please allow me to make it up to you." His voice deepened as he slipped the cloth around her head and tied it.

"You could do that by taking my turn," she suggested.

He leaned toward her, his mouth so close she could feel his breath on her cheek. "I have a better idea. Why don't you let me take you to dinner instead?"

Her heart skidded to a stop. Go out in public with him? Yet why not? Her mind raced. He was a much better companion than Nathan Pierce had turned out to be. He understood her and never tried to dictate to her. She took a step away from

Silas and put her hands out. "Perhaps I will." Then she threw herself into the game to shut out the voice of caution that somehow mimicked the irritating tones of a certain bossy pastor.

fifteen

What was he going to do about his feelings for Abigail? Nathan could barely stand the idea of her going to dinner with Silas. Yet he had absolutely no right to so much as warn her about being too trusting.

Yesterday afternoon he'd returned from getting a drink in the stream when he saw the man tying a blindfold around her head. And leaning forward to whisper in her ear. He wished he'd not been close enough to hear the man's question, but he had. And the words had chased him all through the night and even today as he began to make his round of the area churches. If only he could—

A scream interrupted his thoughts and made Nathan pull up on his horse's reins. Animals in the forest chittered and rustled around him, but that was the only thing he heard. He ran a calming hand on his horse's neck as he waited.

Nothing. Not even raised voices.

Nathan was about to continue on his way when it happened again. Another noise, but this time it sounded more like a moan. Then as he strained his ears, he thought he caught the whistle of a whip. Instinct took over. He tightened his knees and sent his mount into a gallop. Somewhere along this road, someone was in trouble.

As he rounded a bend, a woman came running toward him. He dragged back hard on the reins to keep from running her down. The horse reared and almost unseated him, but after a second or two, Nathan managed to get the frightened animal back under control.

"Please, sir." The woman ran up to him and he saw the

tracks of her tears on her dark cheeks. She was dressed in a shapeless black wool shift, a typical dress of slaves in the South. Her eyes were wide with fear and desperation as her hands grabbed hold of his horse's reins. "Please, oh please, sir. You have to help me. He's going to kill my Abram."

"Where?"

She pointed a shaking finger back the way she'd come. "Hurry."

Nathan could not see anything yet, but he set his horse moving once again. The next bend in the road, however, revealed a scene that burned its way deeply into his heart. A large black man had been tied to an oak tree, his back showing wicked stripes from the bite of a whip.

A tall white man with thick shoulders stood behind him, his arm poised to make yet another stripe on the black man's back. He looked back as Nathan galloped up but turned back to face the black man almost immediately.

"Stop!" Nathan brought his horse up short and dismounted. "What do you think you're doing?"

"Nothing that concerns you." The man brought the whip up.

Nathan strode up to him and grabbed his hand. "Yes, it does concern me. You are killing that man."

"He's not a man. He's my property. I can treat him any way I want to." He sneered at Nathan and jerked his hand free. "Now get on your way before I take exception to your interference."

Shaking his head, Nathan pointed at the bound man, who was moaning and trying desperately to free himself. His shirt hung in tatters from his waist. Blood oozed from several of the stripes across his broad back. "I cannot."

The slave owner dropped his whip and reached for his waist. At first Nathan thought he was going to pull a gun, but then he saw the wicked edge and sharp point of a blade. Immediately he was taken back in time. The forest faded away, becoming the main room at Poe's in Chattanooga.

Nathan froze. His heart stuttered. He could not—must not—kill again. He took a step back and raised his hands. "Let's be reasonable."

"The only reasonable thing to do is move on."

"Please, Master, please." The black woman who had first alerted him to the situation ran up to them. She fell to her knees at the white man's feet. "My Abram didn't mean no harm. He wanted to bring me some flowers. He wasn't trying to run away. I swear it." She threw both arms around the man's legs.

As Nathan watched, the maddened look faded from the slave owner's face. He looked at the whip on the ground, back to the male slave's bleeding back, and finally down to the woman kneeling before him. "I suppose he's learned his lesson."

"Oh yes, Master." The woman looked up, her plea for lenience evident in every line of her body. "Abram done learned it good. I promise he won't do it no more." She let go of his legs but didn't make any move to regain her feet.

Nathan felt sick to the core of his being. He had never realized the true horror of slavery. Had never thought about the control slave owners had over the lives of their property. Property! As if one human had the right to own another.

This was the reason slavery should be outlawed. It was wrong, and he knew it, knew it as surely as he knew that he was a coward. No wonder he had earned Abigail's scorn. He wanted to go to her and apologize.

He watched as the white man cut the bonds on his slave and walked away, never looking back. He jumped on the horse that Nathan had not even realized was tethered nearby. Before he galloped away, however, he did turn back to where the woman was supporting Abram. "Leah, I'll expect to see him in the fields at first light."

"Yes, sir." Leah nodded as she wrapped Abram's arm around her shoulders. "Come along. We've got to get back quick."

Nathan's throat choked as he watched their struggle. The beaten man must outweigh her by at least fifty pounds. He had no idea how far away their home was, but it was evident they would never make it without his intervention.

"Let me help." He grabbed the large man by the waist, trying to avoid the ugly slashes on his back. "We'll get him up on my horse and get the two of you out of here."

Leah's large eyes filled with tears again. "Thank you so much, sir. I don't know what we'd've done if the good Lord hadn't sent you."

"You're the one who saved him."

She shook her head and put a hand on his arm. "I had already begged for him to take pity on my husband, but he didn't pay me no mind. Not till you came by."

Feeling unworthy of the admiration in her gaze, Nathan said nothing. But he knew better. If he'd been any kind of man, he would have wrested the knife away from their master and overcome him. He should have stopped the vicious beating. But he had not been able to do it. He had been silent in the face of his fear. He didn't deserve anyone's admiration.

❧

Nathan's heart broke as he listened to Leah crooning to Abram while dabbing the angry red stripes across his back. These people were being treated like animals—no rights, no hopes, no future. He had never considered what it must be like to live this way.

It had grown quiet in the small cabin. He looked up to see Leah, her shoulders bowed, moving to a shelf on one side of the room. "How is he doing?"

She picked up a jar and carefully poured a small amount

of green powder into her palm. "My Abram is strong. He's suffered a lot in his life. He's gonna git through this hurt, too."

"Is there something I can do to help?"

Leah pursed her lips. "You can take this bowl outside and empty it. There's a spring right at the edge of the woods where we get our fresh water."

Nathan emptied and refilled the bowl as directed. As he walked back toward the little circle of slave cabins, he realized he was the center of attention. Dark faces peered at him from the doorways while children who had been playing outside stopped to watch him. These people obviously had little experience with white men who cared about their needs. Someone had started a cook fire in the open space at the center of the slave quarters. A rough framework of tree limbs next to the dancing flames probably served as a spit for roasting their meat.

Leah and Abram's home was made of weathered gray wood. It had one door, one window, and a dirt floor. It was smaller than some of the other cabins, and he wondered if that was because the couple seemed to have no children.

As he reentered the single room, Leah looked up with a warm smile. She was kneeling next to Abram and had a hand on his forehead. "He has no fever. Your prayers are strong."

Nathan was humbled by the faith shining in her face. It made him feel grasping and greedy to bemoan his trials when he witnessed this woman's gratitude even though she had so few blessings in her life. "I'm glad."

He handed her the bowl and watched as she poured a little of the water into a wooden cup, added the green powder, and stirred briskly before lathering the paste she'd made onto Abram's back. "This will ease his pain and help him to sleep the night so he will be strong enough to work in the fields tomorrow."

As the afternoon sun dipped below the horizon, the adult workers began returning to the slave quarters. A few of the women came by and spoke in low tones to Leah, bringing food for her and her husband to share. Apparently word had spread to them about the events of the day. They looked in Nathan's direction and bobbed their heads. He nodded in return, feeling very small in the face of their thanks.

"Are you hungry?" Leah held out a bowl of stew.

Nathan shook his head. "Abram needs it more than I." He could feel his stomach rumbling. But he had provisions with him—dried berries and strips of salted beef—that he would eat once he made camp.

Kneeling beside the mat where her husband lay, Leah coaxed him to swallow a little of the stew while Nathan watched. Her tenderness and patience with the wounded man raised a yearning within his heart. Although this couple had so little, they still had each other.

How he wished someone special was waiting for him at home. Someone who would shed a tear of empathy when he was hurt and rejoice with him when triumphs came his way. Someone who challenged him to think and yet loved him in spite of his faults.

Leah finished feeding her husband and returned to the handmade table where Nathan sat. "How came you to be on that road today?"

"I travel about, visiting the communities and spreading the Word of the gospel." Nathan's hands felt empty suddenly. He had left his Bible in his saddlebags.

Her face broke into a wide smile. "You're a preacher man?"

He nodded, even though he felt unworthy of the wonder in his voice. "I am."

"Could you tell me a story from your Bible?" Her hands pressed together. "I used to go by the church on Sunday and stand in the door so I'd hear the preacher, but then Master said he didn't want us hanging 'bout and told us to stay home. So it's been awhile since I heared anything."

Verses from Luke's Gospel filled his mind, the words of Jesus as He spoke to the multitudes of followers. It was as if God was reaching down from His throne in heaven and inspiring him. " 'Blessed be ye poor: for yours is the kingdom of God. Blessed are ye that hunger now: for ye shall be filled.' " Nathan could feel the comfort in those words flowing through him. His voice grew stronger as he continued. ' "Blessed are ye that weep now: for ye shall laugh. Blessed are ye, when men shall hate you, and when they shall separate you from their company, and shall reproach you, and cast out your name as evil, for the Son of man's sake. Rejoice ye in that day, and leap for joy: for, behold, your reward is great in heaven. . . .' "

Leah clapped her hands. "I see why you're a preacher."

From the other side of the room, Abram shifted on his pallet. "Them's some good words."

Nathan hadn't even realized the man was conscious, much less that he could absorb the meaning of the words in spite of his pain. He got up from the table and walked over to the corner where Abram lay. "May God's embrace comfort you and His Word give you the strength to overcome the evil of this world." He put his hand on the black man's thick shoulder, careful not to touch his back, bowed his head, and took a deep breath. "Lord, please look down on this man, Abram, and heal him. May he and his wife, Leah, find favor in Your sight. Please grant them freedom. Give them hope for tomorrow and bless them with Your mighty blessings. We know, Lord, that You gave Yourself for our sins, and we thank You most humbly. Amen."

"Amen." Both Abram and Leah repeated the word after him.

"Thank you, Preacher." Leah's voice recalled him from the tumult in his heart.

Nathan felt both diminished and strengthened by what was happening in the meager slave quarters. Never before had he felt so strongly the power of the Lord. Never before had he been swept away by awe and wonder. Never before had God seemed so real to him. The sermons and prayers he'd spoken in the past seemed but a pale version of what had taken place here.

He wanted time alone to consider the ramifications, so he took his leave with promises to return. He also made a promise to himself to do something to help these two escape their bondage. Nathan knew he didn't have enough money to purchase their papers, but he also was beginning to realize God could give him whatever was necessary.

Nathan collected his horse and left the plantation behind. When he found a place to make camp, he gathered pine needles for a bed and settled down. He gazed up into the starlit sky. Was God looking down on him right now? A sense of peace covered him like a warm blanket, and Nathan understood that his question was answered. No matter what had happened in his past, God was still there for him.

His unworthiness brought the sting of tears to his eyes. Nathan drifted to sleep somewhere between regret and thankfulness.

sixteen

"I saw her." Deborah put down her glass of lemonade with a clatter. "I know how ridiculous it sounds, Abigail, but I saw Mrs. Aucoin."

"You're telling me you saw a ghost?"

A nod answered her. "She was dressed in a white flowing robe and carrying a lantern." Deborah reached out and grabbed Abigail's arm. "It had the same green glow the children saw a few weeks ago."

Abigail was dumbfounded. Deborah was not given to flights of fancy. She had been raised in the orphanage and had raised dozens of other children in her turn. She was as practical and capable a person as any Abigail had ever met. And now she was claiming to have seen a ghost.

"I know you remember the story. Robert Aucoin was a pirate who sailed the river and attacked merchants and visitors making their way down to New Orleans. He was caught and hung somewhere around Memphis. When the local authorities came to his wife and told her what had happened, she refused to believe it. She ran from the room, screaming that her husband was a good man who would return to her."

A shiver teased its way down Abigail's spine. She had heard the tales about the poor, crazy woman who walked along the bluff out back, looking for her husband, losing her grasp on sanity when year after year passed without his reappearance. Poor, mad Vanessa Aucoin. Abigail shook herself. "While I'm aware Robert and Vanessa Aucoin were real people who once lived here, no one above the age of twelve really believes they haunt this house. They are only stories children tell because of some ghoulish enjoyment they get from frightening one another."

"I thought so, too, until last week." Deborah let go of her arm and leaned back against the sofa. "I've not been sleeping well, what with the noises the children keep hearing and the lights moving back and forth."

"That must be the explanation." Abigail felt better. Her friend was not becoming unbalanced. "You probably thought you were awake. It's very understandable. What we need to do is hire an assistant for you, someone who can help you with the responsibilities you carry. I come over as often as I can manage, but you need someone else who lives here with you and the children. Then you can get some well-deserved rest."

Deborah shook her head. "I'm sure of what I saw. It was a woman dressed in white. And she had to be a ghost because while I was watching, *poof*"—Deborah clapped her hands for emphasis—"she disappeared like a puff of smoke."

Abigail cast about for some logical explanation. "Perhaps one of the older girls was walking outside."

"No, I checked. For once, all of the children were sleeping peacefully right where they should be." She held up one hand. "And before you suggest one of the neighbors, remember that she disappeared without warning. How could she have done that if she was a real person? The drop down to the river is one hundred feet or more. No one could survive such a fall."

"I don't know, Deborah. But there must be a mundane answer."

"There is. The ghost of Mrs. Aucoin."

Abigail blew out a breath. "I would have to meet her face-to-face before I'd believe that."

"I'd probably feel the same way if you told me the story I've told you, but I know what I saw." She sighed. "Enough of my problems. Why don't you tell me what's been going on with you the past few days?"

The change of subject was abrupt, but Abigail allowed it. She would mention the problem to her parents. They needed to know something odd was going on here. Perhaps they could get to the bottom of the situation.

Abigail sipped at her lemonade as she considered what topic might get Deborah's mind off of her problems. After a moment, she knew what subject to broach. It was sure to remove all thought of apparitions. "I am going to dinner with Mr. Ward on Friday."

That did the trick. Deborah's mouth dropped open. "Mr. Ward has secured your attention? I never would have thought it possible."

"Why do you say that? Mr. Ward is a nice man. He works hard, has an accommodating disposition, and is very considerate of my feelings."

"But I thought your parents had hoped for a match between you and Brother Pierce."

Abigail almost choked on her drink. "Nathan? I cannot think of a worse idea. Brother Pierce is pro-slavery, anti-children, and very domineering."

"Oh my. Well, that would never do." Deborah summoned a weak smile. "But please be careful when you are with Mr. Ward."

"Why do you say that?" Abigail's hand crept up to her throat. "Do you know something unsavory about Mr. Ward?"

"Unsavory?" Deborah looked at a point directly above Abigail's left shoulder. "I wouldn't say that. But there is something about him, something familiar. Yet when I try to pin down the feeling, it slips away from me. I keep thinking I know him, but I know it's impossible." She turned her focus back to Abigail's face. "I wish you hadn't agreed to see him."

Abigail shrugged. "I thank you for your advice, but I am

committed for a dinner. If it makes you feel any better, I will be on my guard."

"I'm certain everything will be fine." Deborah's smile wobbled a bit. "It's probably one more sign I am slipping over the edge of sanity."

"Don't be silly. I'm sure it's a matter of getting enough sleep and relieving your mind of some of the pressures it is under. Once we find someone to assist you, I'm certain you'll feel better in no time."

ॐ

Silas put down his spoon and looked across the linen-covered table. "Is your gumbo tasty?" Abigail brushed her mouth with a starched napkin and nodded. "It's a bit spicy, but I like it that way."

"That's good." He picked up his spoon and dipped it into his bowl once more.

At this rate, dinner was going to be a very long meal. Abigail wondered what topic she could bring up. They had already covered the weather—warm—the number of people dining out nowadays—dozens—and the broad variety of items available at the local mercantile—amazing.

She glanced at Silas and thought that he was at least a well-mannered diner. He did not slurp from his spoon or put his elbows on the dinner table. But other than that, she could not say many favorable things about him. Silas had a knack of agreeing with every statement she uttered. While that should make her feel as though her ideas were correct, Abigail wondered if he might agree even if she now switched her position to the opposite point of view.

"I had a most interesting visitor this morning."

This sounded like the start of a good topic. "Who was that?"

"William Johnson. He said he wanted to meet me and tell me about his shop around the corner from my office."

A spark of interest flared. Abigail looked at Silas with more enthusiasm. Her father had once patronized William Johnson's barbershop. "He is quite famous in this area."

A nod answered her. "He told me a little of his background. How he was freed as a child and learned his trade before purchasing a building downtown and opening his shop. He said he's the barber for many of the landowners in Natchez."

"Yes, his business acumen is extraordinary, but did you know that he himself owns slaves?"

Silas's eyebrows climbed toward his hairline. "Is that so? How odd. One would think that, having been a slave himself, he would oppose slavery."

"Yes, it is shocking to me, too." Abigail sighed. "Papa says it's because of Mr. Johnson's desire for higher social status."

"Your father is very perceptive." Silas leaned forward. "Mr. Johnson wanted to know if I planned to take part in the Fourth of July festivities."

"What did you tell him?"

When his lips curved upward, she tried to convince herself the man sitting on the opposite side of the table was attractive. Some would describe him as dashing, with his dark hair and eyes, but she found his intense gaze a bit off-putting. As he hesitated before giving her an answer, Abigail found herself comparing him to the tall, blond-haired, blue-eyed minister. Somehow, Nathan seemed much more appealing.

"I'm not certain." His voice cut through her wandering thoughts.

Perhaps it was guilt over not giving him her full attention that shaped her answer. "Oh, you must. We have great fun."

"Sometimes they can be quite tedious with speeches from self-serving politicians and ill-mannered children allowed to run loose like heathens."

Abigail's initial excitement faded in response to his words.

Doubt brought her eyebrows together. She thought Silas enjoyed being around children. It was Nathan who was uncomfortable. Or had Silas only been pretending to enjoy the orphans' company for his own reasons?

Tucking the question away for later consideration, she consciously smoothed her expression before answering. "Besides the speeches, we have games, tasting competitions, and boat races along the river. Then everyone gets together to eat watermelon and watch the incredible fireworks display."

His gaze sharpened on her face. He leaned forward slightly. "Will you be attending?"

"Of course." Abigail sat back in her chair, her hand resting next to her empty bowl of gumbo. "My family always goes. Mama's pickled pears usually win the competition for canned fruits, and she's been experimenting with a special recipe to enter into the pie contest this year."

"I may have to sign up to be a judge then." He reached across the table and put his hand on top of hers. "All of a sudden, listening to a few long-winded politicos seems a small price to pay."

Tugging her hand out from under his, Abigail hid it in her lap. "I usually enjoy their speeches, but perhaps I am too dim-witted to give an opinion."

Now it was Silas's turn to furrow his eyebrows. "Please forgive me. I didn't mean to insult you or your celebration. I'm certain it will be an outstanding day. I cannot wait to take part."

Feeling a little foolish for her discomfort, Abigail nodded. "I apologize for my snappish remark. But you should take into consideration that this is my home. I love Natchez, and I hate to hear newcomers disparage our customs."

Their waiter came to their table as she finished speaking, his tray laden with food. Abigail could tell Silas wanted to say something more, but he folded his lips into a tight line and waited as they were served the main course—roast lamb.

"Is there something else I can bring you?" The man smiled at something on the other side of the room.

Abigail shook her head.

"No, thank you." Silas answered for both of them.

As soon as he walked away, Silas's dark gaze returned to her face. "I hope you'll forgive me, Abigail. The thought of losing your friendship is shredding my heart." He put his hand on his chest. "I won't be able to enjoy a single morsel of this dinner unless you accept my apology."

How melodramatic the man was. He ought to be a thespian. He had obviously missed a successful career on the stage. Promising herself to never again be put in a similar situation, Abigail nodded.

Silas stretched his hand out, his fingers beckoning her to put her hand in his.

Abigail would have liked nothing more than to leave the table and take herself home, but she knew it was impossible. So she held onto her temper and forced a smile. "Really, Silas. Please don't make a scene. I accept your apology. You may consider yourself completely forgiven and this whole conversation forgotten."

She ignored his hand and pushed her meat around her plate. Would this evening never end?

seventeen

Nathan heard the singing before he reached Gatlin Camp Ground. It seemed to carry on the wind, like the voices of angels, and he felt hope lifting his spirit as he moved forward.

In the week since he'd left Abram and Leah, his mind had poked and prodded at his long-held acceptance of enslavement. He felt like a man who had lived his whole life in a dark cave—a cavern whose walls were indifference and ignorance. How could he have ever been so blind?

Nathan tightened his knees on his horse's saddle as he began singing along with the unseen worshipers. Crossing the clear waters of Topisaw Creek, he followed a well-marked path to an open area. Several wood cabins clustered together at the far edge of the campground, their backs to the dense woods of pine trees wider around than Nathan was tall. A large structure rose from the ground to his right, its walls nothing more than poles driven into the ground. A crowd of people sat under the interlaced saplings and tree limbs that formed the roof.

Wondering if he should try to stow his gear first or join the others under the brush arbor, Nathan dismounted and led his horse to the corral. He removed his saddle and bags, stacking them to one side of the fence for later retrieval.

"Well, would you look at who's finally come riding in." The lilting voice made his heart race and brought a smile to Nathan's face.

"It's good to see you, Abigail." He took off his hat and bowed to her.

"We got here yesterday." She scuffed at a patch of grass. "It's going to be a great week."

"Yes." Nathan stared at the top of her head, his fingers itching to loosen her chignon. He wanted to wrap his arms around her and kiss her. Thoughts of pressing his lips against her soft mouth robbed him of the ability to speak.

Moments passed until she finally turned her dark gaze up to his face. His feelings must have been apparent on his face because her cheeks reddened. She glanced back toward where the others were still singing. "I'd better get back to the meeting. It looks like Bishop Ross is about to begin his sermon."

"Don't go." The two words shot from his mouth with the velocity of a rifle blast. "I. . .I've been thinking about you a lot. Wondering if you've kept busy." He wanted to bite off his tongue as soon as the words escaped. Would she be able to tell how jealous he'd been? The thought of her being entertained by the officious Silas Ward had stolen several nights of slumber. He squared his shoulders. "I mean, I know how much. . .how many. . ."

A smile teased her mouth. She reached up and pushed the errant lock of hair behind one ear. "Yesterday Mama and I were discussing how quiet it's been at Magnolia lately."

His heartbeat galloped at her words. Was she admitting she'd missed him? Excitement raised the corners of his mouth in an answering smile. "I have something important to tell you and your family."

Her brows drew together. "What is that?"

"I've realized how right you are."

"It's about time." A grin replaced the concern on her face. "Tell me more."

He held out a hand to her. After a moment's hesitation, she placed her own smaller hand in his. Together they walked back to the creek he and his horse had recently crossed.

Nathan led her over to a fallen tree and helped her sit down. He stepped back and took a deep breath. "Slavery is a diabolical practice that has to be eradicated."

Delight caused her dark eyes to glow. "What happened?"

Nathan told her briefly about Abram and Leah.

When he finished, she clapped her hands together. "Praise God for opening your eyes."

"Yes." Nathan picked up a rock and tossed it into the creek. "I cannot believe how blind I was. But that's over now."

Abigail stood up and brushed off her skirt. "I am so glad to hear you've come to your senses."

He nodded. "I'm ashamed of my blindness."

"You're not to blame." She put a hand on his arm. "Our experiences form our opinions. In fact, you're to be commended for refusing to be bound by your preconceptions."

Nathan felt at least twenty feet tall—taller than the trees surrounding them. He looked down at Abigail's earnest face. Should he express his feelings now or wait? Was this the right time? The right place?

She turned away, and he realized his hesitation had cost him the opportunity to speak. Maybe that was best. He had absolutely no idea how to form the right words to win her affection.

"We need to get back to the others." Abigail took a step toward the brush arbor. "My parents will come looking for me if I don't return soon."

He nodded, relieved and yet disappointed the decision had been taken from him. He caught up with her as they reached the campground. "Do you think they'll mind if I don't take time to wash?"

She turned back and looked him over, her gaze serious as it slid from his sweat-dampened hair to his wrinkled shirt. "It's up to you."

Wavering for a moment as the desire to be near her warred

with his need to clean off the dirt of travel, Nathan finally shook his head. "It won't take me long."

Her gaze returned to his face. Was that disappointment he saw? His heartbeat quickened. He took a step forward.

"The cabin at the end of the row is for the single men's use."

Her dismissive words stopped him from reaching for her hand. Hope leeched out of him as she walked away. With a sigh, Nathan picked up his gear and made his way to the cabin Abigail had indicated, as she disappeared into the crowd of worshipers.

The door creaked as he pushed it open. "Is anyone here?" His question met silence.

Wooden bunks filled the room, some with blankets and bags on them, others empty of anything except a thin mattress. He chose one of the latter, sitting down and placing his bags at his feet. After a quick search, he took out a sliver of Colgate soap and a fresh shirt before retracing his steps to the creek. Although he would have enjoyed a full soak in the cool water, he settled for an abbreviated bath before combing his wet hair and tucking the clean white shirt into the waist of his trousers.

Nathan walked back to the brush arbor and tried to slip quietly onto a bench, but the bishop smiled and beckoned him forward. An air of expectation filled the arbor as if the Lord was in this place.

He glanced around the arbor at the smiling faces. Their peace was almost tangible enough to touch. And then he saw Abigail, her face so pure, so radiant, so filled with adoration for the Lord. In that moment, Nathan knew he must become like the people before him. He had to find the same relationship for himself.

❧

"The poem is called 'Just As I Am,' and it has a powerful

message, one I'd like to share with all of you this evening."
Brother Oliver Smith had taken the podium for the final
evening of the revival. " 'Just as I am without one plea. . .' "

At first mesmerized by the reading of the powerful poem,
Abigail found herself glancing toward Nathan sitting next
to her. He had been so serious this week. He'd spent hours
talking to the bishop and her father, reading his Bible, and
even teaching parables to the children. She would have liked
to spend more time talking to him, but with so much going
on, it had been impossible. It seemed the only time they sat
near each other was under the arbor where they could not
talk.

He seemed to have won the admiration of everyone here,
especially the ladies. And why not? She admired the firm
angle of his jaw, his pronounced cheekbones, blue eyes, and
thick blond hair. A man ought not be so handsome. Add
to that his nice manners, kindness, and consideration of the
feelings of others. Who could resist him?

" 'Here for a season, then above, O Lamb of God, I come, I
come!' " The preacher's voice rang out, drawing her attention
back where it belonged. She hoped no one noticed how red
her cheeks had become.

"Jesus is waiting to claim you as His own. He doesn't want
to wait until you get your life all straightened out. No, sir.
He wants you to come to Him just as you are. I'm going
to talk to you tonight about the first time I heard someone
reading these powerful words. They changed me. Made me a
different man than the one you see standing up here tonight."

The emotion of the preacher's voice pulled on Abigail. She
listened to his story about being a thief, a robber who preyed
on travelers along the Natchez Trace. As he spoke, she could
feel the Lord's presence with them.

"One of my victims was a Christian man. He prayed for
me even when I took his money. Even though I laughed at

his weakness, this man continued asking for Jesus to forgive me. I wish I could tell you that his faith turned me from my life of crime, but it didn't. I went on my way, certain he was a fool. Then about two weeks later I was visiting my ma up in Jackson, and she talked me into going to her church. While I was there, I heard that poem for the very first time."

He stopped speaking and stood in front of them silently for a moment. " 'Just as I am, and waiting not, to rid my soul of one dark blot.' Now I can tell you I had a lot of dark blots on me and in me. More blots than most." Brother Smith held up the sheet of paper, and Abigail could see the deep creases in it and the stain of what looked like tears. "But I could hear Jesus' voice as though He was standing right there in front of me. His blood cleanses each and every spot. What could I say except, 'O Lamb of God, I come, I come.'"

Tears stung at her eyes, and Abigail reached for her reticule. That's when she realized Nathan was no longer sitting next to her. He had fallen to his knees in front of the bench, his hands clasped in front of him. His head was bowed, his lips were moving. He might be a preacher, but tonight he was meeting the Lord as though for the first time.

Her breath caught and a tear escaped to roll down her cheek. It was not a tear of remorse, but one of joy. What an inspiring thing to see Nathan crossing the line between a man of character to a man of abiding faith.

The preacher ended his sermon with an invitation to everyone to go to the creek for baptisms. Nathan was one of the first ones to meet him in the center of the creek where the water was nearly waist deep, eager to renew his dedication to the Lord with another baptism.

Abigail clasped her hands together under her chin and watched as he submitted to the preacher. Watched as his blond head went under the water. Applauded with the others when he was raised up again, the water sluicing off of him in rivulets. She was standing right at the edge of the water as he waded out, the first to congratulate him.

"Abigail. . .I suppose you're wondering—"

She quieted him with a glance. "Isn't it wonderful to be sure of your place in heaven?"

"Yes." A broad smile creased his face, making him more handsome than ever. "Yes, it is."

Her parents came over then, taking their turns talking to him and congratulating him on renewing his faith. What a wonderful day it had turned out to be, and the perfect way to end a week of revival.

eighteen

Nathan accepted Mr. LeGrand's offer to tie his horse to the rear of the wagon and ride back with the family. Even though Abigail had already heard about his change of heart, she listened with attention as he shared the story of Abram and Leah with her parents. He hesitated once when trying to describe the emotions he'd experienced, and she slipped her hand in his.

The squeeze of her fingers almost took his breath away, but he recovered his equilibrium after a moment and continued. "I was arrogant and ignorant, a dangerous combination. Now I want to do something to make up for my wrongheadedness."

"I told him he was to be commended for seeing the truth when he did." Abigail's dark gaze fluttered over him like the gentle touch of a butterfly's wing. She pulled her hand away from his as her father slowed the wagon.

Her mother glanced over her shoulder and smiled at both of them. "She's right. Of course we know that God does not ask us to make reparations, only to do better now that we have been made into new creatures."

As Mr. LeGrand brought the wagon to a full stop, Nathan considered Mrs. LeGrand's statement. He was beginning to realize the truth of her words, and it gave him a feeling of freedom, as though a heavy burden had been lifted from his shoulders. If he held out his arms, he might fly right off the back of the wagon.

"Why are we stopping, Papa?"

Mr. LeGrand pointed toward a glade a few feet away. "This looks like a good place to have our lunch."

Nathan jumped down from the wagon and turned to help Abigail. Then he and Mr. LeGrand spread a blanket on the ground under the shade of an oak tree and waited while the ladies laid out their food. Fried chicken, pickles, and carrots were passed around, followed by a selection of fresh fruits.

As soon as they finished eating, he broached the subject that he felt must be discussed. "I know all of you must wonder about a preacher needing to be baptized."

"Alexandra and I discussed that subject last night after we retired, but we didn't think it was our place to ask about such things." Mr. LeGrand crossed his legs at the ankle and leaned back on one elbow. "Your relationship with the Lord is a private matter."

"I've heard of people who have been baptized several times." Mrs. LeGrand shrugged. "I told Jeremiah you were probably carried away by the sermon and decided to reaffirm your faith in a public way."

"I suppose that was part of it." Nathan stood and brushed a crumb off his shirtsleeve. "But I have also been guilty of deceit—to myself and to you good people."

"What do you mean?" Abigail shaded her eyes with one hand.

"I am a murderer."

Abigail and her mother gasped.

Mr. LeGrand sat up straight. "What are you talking about?"

"The reason I became a preacher was to make amends for killing someone. I was trying to protect a friend of mine and things got ugly. The attacker and I struggled, and he pulled a knife, but he slipped and fell on the blade." Nathan flexed his hand. "I can still feel the horror of that moment."

Shocked silence greeted him.

Nathan turned away and walked up a slight rise. He wanted to give the LeGrands time to absorb his story and decide whether or not they should continue to offer him their hospitality.

A pond on the other side of the hill reflected the blue, cloudless sky. He meandered toward it, wondering if the LeGrands would forgive him. He could understand if they did not. It had taken him a long time to forgive himself.

He picked up a rock and tossed it in the water. Ripples broke up the smooth surface of the water much like his words had disturbed the peace of his hosts. He sighed and glanced upward. At least he still had the comfort of his Savior. He would lend Nathan the fortitude to saddle his horse and ride back alone. Perhaps he could even be packed up by the time Abigail's family made it home.

A hand touched the small of his back and Nathan whirled around. "Abigail."

"I think you're the bravest man I've ever met." The admiration in her dark gaze warmed him through.

Nathan cleared his throat. "You amaze me, Abigail LeGrand. You have an infinite ability to surprise me. Being around you makes me feel like the most fortunate man alive. I cannot believe you and your family have forgiven me."

"Why not?" She smiled at him. "We can see what kind of man you are. You didn't have to tell us, you know. The very fact that you did proves how honorable you are."

Humility swept through him. This woman believed in him. She was a treasure to him, a miracle. He knew beyond a doubt that she was the only woman he would ever love.

Nathan bent down on one knee and took her hand in his. "Abigail, I once thought I loved a woman, but the feelings I had toward her are nothing but a wisp of smoke when compared to what I feel when I'm around you."

"Get up, Nathan." Abigail tried to pull her hand away. "I don't want to embarrass you, but there's no way I can let you go any further."

When he was a young boy, he'd once strayed into a neighbor's field and been discovered by the man's bull. The aggressive animal had charged him and butted him in the stomach. The pain of that day returned to him in full force as she spoke.

But then he looked up into Abigail's face and saw the sheen of tears in her eyes. Her expression was saying the exact opposite of her words. She cared for him.

"I have to go further, Abigail. This is too important. I have to find out why you're not being honest with me." When he realized how hard she was pulling on her hand, he released it.

She staggered back but caught her balance. "I. . .it's just that I have been raised different from other women." She wiped at the tears that tracked down her cheeks. "I cannot imagine trying to submit to you the way a good wife should."

If she hadn't been crying, he would have laughed out loud. Instead he stood up and closed the distance between them. He put a gentle hand on her shoulder. "Do you think I'm stupid?"

"What?" Her mouth fell open and her tears stopped falling. "Oh. . .of course not."

Nathan let his hand trail from her shoulder to her cheek. "Abigail LeGrand, you are the least submissive woman I've ever met. I love you because of who you are. Your intelligence, your honesty, your unflagging spirit—those are the things I admire about you. The way you always seek to help others. The way you give yourself, heart and soul, to whatever cause inspires you. I don't need some dull, drab female to clean my house and follow my orders. I need a helpmeet. I need you."

Abigail's breath caught, and a look of wonder filled her face. For a moment he thought he'd convinced her, but then the light in her eyes dimmed. She shook her head slowly.

He knew she was about to turn him down. Nathan also knew he could not let her say the words. Once they were spoken, it would be hard for his hardheaded love to retract them. So he put a finger on her lips. "Shhh. I know I've surprised you, but I want you to think about what I've said. Abigail, I want you to pray about it. Take your time. You'll find I am a patient man."

nineteen

"I'm ready." Abigail's pink skirt swirled around her feet as she descended the stairs. She swung her matching parasol from one gloved finger and wondered why she didn't feel more excited about the day ahead. She always enjoyed the town's Fourth of July celebration. But this year she found herself pensive about what the day would bring.

It had been nearly two weeks since Nathan had proposed, and she still didn't know what answer to give him. The question had been uppermost in her mind no matter what she was doing. The children at the orphanage hadn't noticed her preoccupation, but Deborah had teased her mercilessly when she pulled a rose from a vase and tried to write a note with it.

She saw Nathan in the pulpit on Sunday, but he had not been over to visit her or her parents since they'd gotten back from the revival meeting. Was he regretting his impulsive proposal? Or giving her time to be certain of whatever answer she decided to give him?

Nathan's words of love and devotion had awakened a longing in her, and she was beginning to think the only solution was to accept his proposal. The idea of submitting to his will had even begun to seem less abhorrent. Perhaps the bishop's wife had been speaking the truth all those weeks ago in Jackson when she said it would be easy to submit to a man who loved her as much as Christ loved the Church.

Mama was waiting at the foot of the stairs. The look she bent on her daughter made Abigail check with a nervous hand to make sure her coiffure was straight. "Is something wrong?"

"Why don't you tell me?"

Mama's smile sent color rushing to Abigail's cheeks. "I don't know what you're talking about."

She walked outside to find her father talking to none other than the man who had been uppermost on her mind for two whole weeks. He wore freshly creased trousers, a black coat, and a crisp white shirt. His blond hair was brushed back from his face, but one lock had rebelled and fallen across his forehead, giving him a dashing look. His blue eyes shone as though lit from within, and a warm smile turned his lips up. Odd how a simple glance at him made her heart speed up. "Nathan. . .I didn't expect to see you."

Papa laughed out loud at her social gaffe as Nathan swept a bow. "Your father asked me to drive one of the wagons. Would you like to ride with me to the orphanage?"

Without a glance for permission from either of her parents, Abigail put out her hand. "I would enjoy that immensely."

As soon as Nathan helped her up, he joined her on the bench. "It's a beautiful day, isn't it?"

"Yes, it's perfect for the celebration." She reached for her parasol and opened it.

"I was worried because of the storms last week."

Abigail watched his strong hands as he handled the reins. "I've been thinking about what you said to me that day."

"I'm glad to hear that." His voice was wry. "I'd hate to think you had forgotten my proposal."

She couldn't help the giggle his words and tone caused. But the laughter fled a moment later when he stopped the wagon. "What are you doing?"

He took her parasol from her hand and closed it. "Something I've regretted not doing that day."

His blue gaze was like a caress. He placed his hands on either side of her face and leaned toward her. His lips brushed hers lightly. . .then with more insistence. His touch was sweeter than a song. It made her feel precious, feminine, beloved. It was the most wonderful thing she had ever experienced in her life. She almost reached out to pull him near again when he ended the kiss.

"I love you, Abigail." His voice shook slightly, as though he was as affected by the kiss as she had been. "Please tell me you'll marry me."

All of her doubts melted away like frost at sunrise. Abigail put a hand over her thundering heart and tried to swallow, but her mouth was dry as dust. She couldn't force out a single syllable. So she nodded.

Nathan gathered her in his arms and hugged her. "You've made me the happiest man on earth." He kissed her again. And again.

Finally she pushed at his chest. "We have to go get the children."

"What children?" He placed a kiss at the base of her neck.

Abigail giggled. "The ones at the orphanage. They're waiting for us."

He sighed and straightened. "I suppose you're right."

All the way into town she drank in his profile and sent silent prayers of gratefulness to God for bringing them together.

&

"Where's Mia?" Abigail put a hand on her hip. "She was playing jackstraw earlier, but no one has seen her for a while."

Nathan was sitting cross-legged on the ground, playing marbles with some of the boys from the orphanage. She had watched him all afternoon as he talked and played with the children. They all loved him, and he no longer looked as though he was being skinned when they crowded around him. The change in him was one she could definitely live with.

He unfolded his legs and stood up, brushing at the dirt

that had accumulated on his pants. "I don't know."

"I'm worried she went back to the orphanage to check on Boots." Mia had pouted when they refused to let her bring the orphanage cat along. Abigail had tried to explain that a kitten would be frightened by all the noise and people, but Mia had refused to budge until Nathan stepped in and convinced her to let Boots take a nap while they went to the festivities. Mia had acted fine once she got to the town square, but she could have slipped off to collect Boots when their backs were turned. "I've already asked around," Abigail continued, "but no one has seen her for the past hour."

Nathan reached for the coat he'd draped over a nearby tree limb. "I'll go to the orphanage and look for her."

"I'll go with you." She looked toward the stable. "Why don't we walk and save the time it would take to get the wagon hitched?"

He held out his arm, and she put her hand on it, blushing slightly at the unexpected tingle caused by his nearness. They walked down the street, smiling and nodding at the people they passed. It seemed everyone in Natchez was here.

Vendors had set up temporary booths selling everything from melons to barbecued ribs. Politicians shook hands and talked about the challenges facing Mississippi. Children shouted and ran through the crowds, playing games of tag or hide-and-seek while their parents looked on from the shade of the large trees ringing the town square. Once the sun set, families would enjoy watching the fireworks before they returned to their homes.

Nathan put his hand over Abigail's. "I may owe Mia my thanks since her disappearance has given me an excuse to be alone with you."

She sliced a glance at him from the corner of her eye. "You're going to make me wonder if it was your idea for her to go back to the orphanage."

His laughter rang out on the still air. "I am crushed to be so misunderstood."

It felt so good when her laugh joined his. Their life together was going to be full of wonderful moments. They walked on in perfect harmony, leaving the crowds behind. If not for her concern about Mia, Abigail would have been content to have their walk last for hours.

"When can we get married?"

The question sizzled through her. "We haven't even told my parents yet."

"We can do that tonight." He raised his eyebrows and waggled them.

Abigail giggled. "I think a Christmas wedding would be romantic."

"Christmas!" He shook his head. "I think July would be much better."

"Let's worry about that once we collect Mia." A frown replaced Abigail's smile as they approached the orphanage. "It doesn't look like anyone is here."

"I think I see a light." Nathan pointed at an odd green glow that seemed to emanate from the backyard.

The ghost! Was it possible? They skirted the outside of the house as the sun dipped below the horizon. The sight that met her eyes made Abigail's blood freeze. A figure in a long white robe moved silently along the edge of the bluff, waving a green-tinted lantern back and forth.

After the first second of disbelief passed, anger swelled inside her. She recognized the arrogant strut of the so-called ghost. What was Silas Ward doing out here? And why was he wearing that robe? Was he using the legend of the pirate's wife for some nefarious purpose? His green-shuttered lantern illuminated a mound in the grass and her breath caught. Mia. With a little cry, she pulled away from Nathan and rushed forward. "What have you done?"

Silas looked up as she ran toward him, his face twisted in a mask of hatred. When Abigail would have knelt to check the little girl, he grabbed her arm and whipped her around so she stood with her back to him. "Where is it?"

"What are you talking about, Silas?" Abigail grimaced as he pushed her arm upward. "Ouch, you're hurting me."

"Let go of her!" Nathan's voice was harsh as he moved toward them.

"Stay back!" Silas pulled a knife from the pocket of his ridiculous robe and pressed it against Abigail's neck.

Nathan stopped abruptly. The blood drained from his face. "What do you want, Silas?"

"I want the treasure. Where is it?" The man holding her sounded crazed.

"What treasure?" She could hear the shock in Nathan's voice.

Silas snorted. "Don't be stupid. This house used to belong to a pirate who hid his treasure here. I've been looking for it, but I haven't found anything. . .yet."

Abigail kept her head still to avoid the prick of his knife. "How do you know about the treasure?"

"I lived here as a child. One of your father's poor orphans. I used to spend hours exploring, looking for the treasure. But then my cousin came to claim me. He took me away and introduced me to the world of drinking and gambling. What a life. . .until the money ran out."

His laughter was harsh. "I even thought about marrying you, but that wouldn't work. You may be rich, but your parents have spoiled you far too much. And you're rather plain, too. Besides, I require obedience from my women."

If the moment had not been so serious, she would have laughed at his words. How ironic that she'd thought this man admired her independence. A movement at her feet caught Abigail's attention.

Mia put a hand on her head and moaned. "What happened?" Her voice was groggy.

Abigail hoped the child was not hurt. It was hard to tell in the weird glow of the green lamp. She looked at it closely.

Silas must have realized her confusion. "It's made from green mica. Useful when you need to imitate a spirit. You should have heard that silly matron going on and on about seeing me out here. All I had to do was blow out the lamp and pull off this robe to disappear. Ingenious, isn't it?"

"You were the one scaring the children?"

Silas pulled her away from Mia and the lamp. "Too bad there wasn't much of value inside the orphanage." The knife bit her neck. "Tell me where the treasure is."

"Don't be an idiot. There's no treasure." She put all the conviction she could muster into the words. "We found a sea trunk hidden behind a false wall in the dining room years ago, but it only held letters and a few trinkets."

She could hear the rage in the hiss of his breath at her ear. "You're lying."

A trickle eased down her neck, and Abigail realized she was bleeding. She looked across at Nathan and forced herself to smile. Whether she lived or died tonight, she would always be thankful to have won his love.

Mia picked that moment to push to her feet and run toward Nathan. Silas loosened his hold on her arm. Instead of trying to pull away, Abigail tripped and fell forward, a moan of pain slipping out as her knees made contact with the hard ground.

❧

Nathan froze for an instant before instinct took over. He leaped forward.

Silas started to haul Abigail back to her feet but released her as he saw Nathan barreling toward him. Nathan ducked as the deadly blade slashed the air, but he came up swinging both arms. His first blow made contact with Silas's jaw. The impact shuddered down the length of his arm and made his stomach roil.

The other man's head snapped back, but he didn't lose his footing. His left fist somehow found its way into Nathan's stomach. Nathan's jaw clenched against the pain radiating outward from his midsection, but he knew he could not afford to double over. Silas was lifting the knife above his head now, holding it in both hands as though wielding an axe. Immediately on the defensive, Nathan grabbed Silas's wrists and pushed hard to keep the blade from biting into his shoulder.

Little by little, Nathan realized he was losing the struggle as the blade inched down. He sent a prayer heavenward for the strength to overcome the madman.

He could not win against the downward force of the knife, but Nathan realized he didn't need to. Instead of trying to stop the blade's descent, he relaxed briefly. A triumphant leer of success lit Silas's features when Nathan's grip weakened. But it changed to horror as Nathan twisted to one side. The blade whizzed harmlessly through the air past his shoulder.

Before Silas could recover, Nathan bent down and thrust his shoulder into the other man's abdomen. Silas tumbled backward, arms windmilling as he teetered on the edge of the steep bluff. A shrill scream tore free as he realized he would not be able to save himself, and he disappeared from Nathan's horrified gaze.

It couldn't happen again. He could not break the sixth commandment again. Anguish and remorse filled him.

He didn't even remember Abigail until she flung her arms around him. "I'm so glad you're safe."

Mia ran to them, apparently unharmed. "You did it, Pastor. You saved us. That was a mean man." She hugged him with nearly as much strength as Abigail had.

"Are you two okay?"

They both nodded, looking at him like he was a hero. So why did he feel like a villain? The question went unanswered as wind gusted against his face.

Wait. Had he heard a cry for help?

Nathan disengaged the clinging arms and flung himself to the ground, his head hanging over the edge of the steep bluff. At first he saw nothing in the failing light, but then a movement below made him catch his breath. "Abigail, Mia, go find a rope. Quick."

They ran toward the house as he reached down for Silas's hand. If he could only reach a few more inches. Nathan strained to no avail. "Hold on. We'll help you."

A loud noise brought his head up. A cascade of red sparks lit the sky. The fireworks had begun.

"Why?" The word was tossed up toward him from the man who was hanging on to life by a thread. "Why are you helping me?"

"Because God loves you. He's perfect, and He loves you in spite of the evil you would commit. How can I do less?"

Silence answered him. Nathan closed his eyes and prayed for Silas to live. Tense moments passed—each one like a fading heartbeat. He considered half-a-dozen plans but rejected all of them.

Finally he heard someone running toward him. He turned his head and saw Abigail. She didn't have a rope, but a sheet billowed around her. What a resourceful woman.

She skidded to a stop next to him. "I sent Mia back to the celebration to get Papa and the sheriff." She lay down next to him and dropped one end of the sheet over the edge of the bluff.

Realizing he would need to anchor the material, Nathan grabbed the other end and sat up. He looped the soft cloth around his waist and tied it in a quick knot. "You're going to have to use the sheet like a ladder, Silas."

A jerk told him Silas had grabbed hold. As the pressure around his waist increased, Nathan wondered if he could stop both of them from plunging to their deaths. As Silas climbed upward, Nathan's boots inched closer to the edge.

As if from a distance, he heard Abigail crying and praying and wished he could comfort her. His jaw clenched as one of his boots slid off the grassy edge into nothingness. He gritted his teeth and tried to hold on.

Shouts sounded. He could feel the pounding of heavy footfalls. Then strong hands grabbed him under his arms and pulled back. Help had arrived in the nick of time.

Someone heaved Silas over the edge, and the terrible pressure around Nathan's waist eased. He stood up slowly as the sheriff placed handcuffs on Silas.

Abigail ran to him and threw her arms around his neck. She kissed his cheek, his ear, his other cheek—her lips trembling against his skin. He held her close and thanked God for preserving all three of them.

Mr. LeGrand's voice brought Nathan back to his senses. "I suppose this means your mother was right."

He tried to disengage himself from Abigail's embrace, but she clung to him like a limpet. Finally he looked over her head and smiled at her father. "I hope you will allow me to marry your daughter, sir."

"Don't be silly, Nathan." Abigail smiled up at him, her dark eyes hinting mischief. "Mama and Papa probably knew before we did that we were in love." She pulled his face down and kissed him soundly.

twenty

"I still can't believe Silas Ward was hiding his past and his true reason for coming to Natchez. If only he had told us the truth, so much pain and misery could have been avoided." Abigail shook her head as she guided the buggy toward the orphanage.

"He was the proverbial wolf in sheep's clothing." Nathan's sigh was lengthy and deep. "I'm glad we stopped him before his plans did any more harm."

"Thanks to your efforts." A thrill of pleasure lifted the corners of her mouth at the expression on Nathan's face. He was such a good man. In the weeks since the revival she had seen him guiding others, loving them in spite of their weaknesses and leading them to Christ by his humble example. How had she ever thought him overbearing or controlling? Christ's love shone through his words and deeds.

This trip to the orphanage was another indication of the changes in this man. He had planned this visit and asked her to join him instead of the other way around. His relationship with several of the children warmed her heart.

As they turned the corner, Nathan pointed toward the orphanage. "We are not the only visitors this morning."

Abigail frowned at the unfamiliar carriage and horses. "It looks like they've come some distance."

Nathan jumped down as soon as she brought the buggy to a halt. "Did your father say anything before you left?"

Tossing the reins to him, she shook her head. "No."

A couple of the boys were chasing each other around the orphanage yard as Nathan helped her dismount, then opened the gate. Before they could make their way to the front porch, the door flew open and Mia appeared with a squeal of delight.

She dashed down the steps and barreled into Nathan, who caught her up in a strong hug. "You seem overly delighted to see me this morning." He planted a kiss on her forehead.

"You'll never believe who has come to us."

Abigail smiled to see the two of them together. They looked so natural.

"I have cousins." Mia's words ended her speculation. "And an aunt and uncle. They've come from Boston to find me." The little girl scrunched up her face for a moment as she gazed at the man holding her. "Is that a long way from Natchez?"

"Yes, it is." Nathan's deep voice carried a hint of sadness. He let Mia slide down as they reached the porch steps. "But I'm sure you'll like it there."

She smiled and ran back inside.

Abigail caught up with Nathan and touched his elbow. "Are you okay?"

A slight grin turned up one side of his mouth. "Of course. I'm thrilled for Mia."

They walked inside together and headed for the parlor, following Mia's excited voice. "And he told me all about how Jesus loves little girls and boys."

Abigail saw Nathan's smile widen. A prayer of thankfulness filled her. They entered the parlor to find a young family inside.

The lady looked much like Mia's mother, petite and fine-boned. Her husband, a shorter, slightly rotund gentleman, was equally well-dressed and wore a pleasant expression as he stood. Their two children, a boy who looked to be a few years older than Mia and a young girl who had to be about her age, sat quietly and listened to their newfound cousin.

Mia performed the introductions—Uncle C. J. and Aunt Dorothy Ogden, and her cousins, Master Patrick and Miss Ruthanne.

"Mia says you are from Boston." Abigail glanced at Nathan, who sat next to her on the sofa.

"Yes." Mrs. Ogden picked at the material of her gown. "I am ashamed to admit that my sister, Mia's mother, and I were estranged almost a decade ago. The reason is not important now, but you can imagine my sorrow at learning of my sister's death. We left when we received the letter telling us about Mia." The warm glance she lavished on the young girl was enough to calm some of Abigail's concerns.

Deborah entered the parlor, a box in her arms. "Hello, Abigail, Brother Nathan. Isn't it a glorious morning?"

The men stood up again, even young Patrick, showing he had been raised properly. The next hour was filled with conversation as they learned everything there was to know about Mia's long-lost relatives. They spoke to Nathan about their church at home and their faith. They talked to Abigail and Deborah about education and a stable home.

By the time the Ogdens readied themselves to leave, Abigail felt reassured about Mia's future. It was still hard to hug Mia for the final time. She would miss the adorable little girl. A glance at Nathan's face told her he also had conflicting feelings.

After Mia finished her good-byes, Miss Ruthanne took her hand. "We're going to have so much fun. You'll love Boston."

Abigail touched Nathan's hand and offered him a smile. "She'll be so much happier."

"Yes, you're right." He brushed a hand across his face, his gesture melting her heart. How wonderful to be in love with someone so caring.

❧

Deborah's sigh broke the silence in the parlor as she picked up a platter of freshly baked sugar cookies. "I highly recommend these, Brother Pierce."

He glanced at the plate of sweets, but his answer was forestalled by Abigail's gasp.

"Is that your bracelet?" Abigail pointed to their hostess's outstretched arm.

"Yes, the sheriff returned it to me." Deborah moved the platter to her other hand and showed them the treasured piece of jewelry. "It seems the vile Mr. Ward must have taken it at some time when he was sneaking about."

Nathan shook his head. "What a shame."

"If not for your bravery, Mr. Ward might never have been stopped." Abigail's voice was filled with admiration.

Nathan tried not to squirm, but it was difficult. God had given him peace over his actions—even if it meant taking another life, he had the responsibility to defend those who needed his help—but he was thankful not to have been the inadvertent cause of yet another man's death. There was still hope for Silas's salvation. "I have visited Mr. Ward twice since that night, and I believe he is coming to the point of listening to God's plan."

The glance from Abigail made him want to squirm even more. He was not worthy of the love he saw in her gaze.

"Isn't it about time for us to go back to Magnolia Plantation?" He hoped she would not see through his bid to distract her.

Abigail raised an eyebrow. "You shouldn't be so modest."

"Don't give him a hard time, Abigail." The laughter in Deborah's voice told him she was not fooled, either. "I wish more men were as humble as Brother Pierce."

Wondering if his ears were as red as they were warm, Nathan led Abigail to the buggy and helped her get settled on the seat before handing her the reins and taking his place beside her.

"Why don't you drive?" She handed him the reins. "I have something much more interesting to do."

He shrugged and guided the horse along the street. "What would that be?"

"Admiring the man I'm going to marry." She tucked her hand around his arm. "Mia is going to be all right, you know."

"Yes." It never ceased to amaze him how perceptive Abigail was. "In the last few days I was wondering if we could adopt her ourselves. But Christ had a better plan in mind."

He loved the way her cheeks reddened. "You are such a special man. I cannot believe how blessed I am to have you in my life."

"And I you." Now it was his turn to blush. "I thank God for you daily."

"I once thought it would be impossible to submit to a man." Her lemony perfume filled his senses as she leaned against his shoulder. "But that was before I knew a man who submitted himself so easily to Christ."

He knew the Scripture she referred to but was curious for her understanding of the subject. "What do you mean?"

"I have always considered myself independent. I thought it a weakness to rely on any man as I've seen so many simpering ladies do."

He couldn't help but interject, "But what about your mother with your father? I wouldn't consider her to be 'simpering.'"

"And neither do I. In fact, it was during a discussion with Mama and Mrs. Ross in Jackson that I really began to see the idea of submitting in a different way. When Mrs. Ross mentioned the words from Paul that I quoted earlier, I began to think that submitting to the right man, the right *godly* man, could indeed be what is intended for a man and wife. Then when I had dinner with Silas, I knew almost immediately I could never submit to him, not even truly respect him."

"So what ultimately changed your mind?"

"You did."

"Me? How?"

"Well, it was actually God working through you. When I witnessed your encounter with God at the campground, I finally understood what Paul meant. I knew I could submit to someone who loved me like Christ loved the Church. You've always wanted only the best for me and have never tried to control me. I love only you and trust you with my heart."

"Hmm, sounds as if we should go camping many more times." He couldn't keep his face serious enough to hide his grin.

Abigail elbowed him in the side. "All right now, where is that Christlike love?"

"Right where you know it to be." He pointed to his chest. "In my heart."

She planted a quick kiss on his cheek. "Same here."

Although he would have liked to bask in the glow of her admiration, Nathan knew it was time to let her see his own weakness. "I didn't start preaching for the right reason."

She sat up and a frown creased her brow. "What are you talking about?"

"Do you remember when I told you and your parents about killing Ira Watson?"

He felt rather than saw her nod.

"I decided the only way to pay for my actions would be to dedicate myself to preaching God's Word. I thought I could earn forgiveness. It wasn't until the night at the campground when I heard that poem about coming to God, 'Just As I Am,' that I realized the truth. No one can earn forgiveness. It's a gift given freely when Christ laid down His life for our sins." The words had come slowly at first, but now they seemed easier. "I thought about quitting. But God kept putting people in front of me, people who seemed to need my help to find their way to Him. People like the slaves I told you about. Even Silas Ward. People who are hurting and lost. And now that I have turned my life over to God without reservation, I believe He has given me the ability to reach them."

Her hands covered his on the reins, and she pulled the horse to a stop. "I love you, Nathan Pierce. And I know you're right. God has something very special in mind for you."

He glanced around and realized they had not quite reached Magnolia Plantation, so he caught her up in his embrace. "I love you, too, Abigail LeGrand. With your support, I know I'll be able to meet every challenge." He pressed his lips against her softer ones, his heart filling with love and thankfulness to have won the admiration of such a special woman. As their kiss deepened, he made a promise to himself to always treasure her love as much as he did at this moment.

epilogue

Nathan stood proudly and watched as Jeremiah LeGrand escorted his daughter down the aisle. This was the happiest day of his life.

Abigail stepped close to him, a wide smile on her face. He could barely believe this vibrant woman was about to become his wife. He sent a silent prayer of thanks heavenward. God had blessed him so. She was especially lovely today, her hair piled high on her head, the white skirt of her dress floating around her. All she needed was a pair of wings to qualify as an angel.

Outside the church, the weather was not as sunny as he'd hoped. A storm had blown in as they were getting ready to leave Magnolia Plantation. But at least it had not stopped anyone from attending.

He glanced toward the pews where the children from the orphanage sat. It seemed odd not to see Mia's expressive face among them, but he had received a letter from her describing her new home. She was being well cared for, so he could not be sad. He would have to remember to send her a letter describing the wedding.

Several people in the packed church gasped as lightning flashed outside, almost immediately followed by the boom of thunder. The wind blew against the walls of the church, but inside peace and love filled the air.

Nathan watched Abigail's face as he repeated his vows of loyalty and love. Then it was her turn. Her voice was hesitant at first but gained strength as she continued.

"Ladies and gentlemen, I now present to you the Reverend

and Mrs. Nathan Pierce."

Instead of going outside, Abigail and Nathan stood next to each other and greeted their friends and neighbors. By the time they had spoken to all of their well-wishers, the sun had come out once more. Nathan wondered if he would ever get used to the rapid weather changes in this part of the country.

Abigail's father went to the podium to get everyone's attention. "We are going to move this celebration to Magnolia Plantation. We have plenty of food for everyone there."

Nathan escorted Abigail to the carriage as a spattering of raindrops fell on them.

She ducked her head and hurried into the vehicle. "I knew we should wait for cold weather."

Nathan climbed in and sat beside her. "I couldn't wait even one more day for you." Putting an arm around her waist, he pulled her close for a kiss. He still could not quite believe the love flowing between them. God had truly blessed them.

Satisfaction and joy filled her face as she broke free for a moment. "Nor I for you, my love."

A Letter To Our Readers

Dear Reader:

In order that we might better contribute to your reading enjoyment, we would appreciate your taking a few minutes to respond to the following questions. We welcome your comments and read each form and letter we receive. When completed, please return to the following:

Fiction Editor
Heartsong Presents
PO Box 719
Uhrichsville, Ohio 44683

1. Did you enjoy reading *Among the Magnolias* by Diane T. Ashley Aaron McCarver?
   ❏ Very much! I would like to see more books by this author!
   ❏ Moderately. I would have enjoyed it more if

   _____

   _____

   _____

2. Are you a member of **Heartsong Presents**? ❏ Yes ❏ No
   If no, where did you purchase this book? _____

   _____

3. How would you rate, on a scale from 1 (poor) to 5 (superior), the cover design? _____

4. On a scale from 1 (poor) to 10 (superior), please rate the following elements.

   ____ Heroine   ____ Plot
   ____ Hero   ____ Inspirational theme
   ____ Setting   ____ Secondary characters

5. These characters were special because? _____

_____

_____

6. How has this book inspired your life? _____

_____

_____

7. What settings would you like to see covered in future
   Heartsong Presents books? _____

_____

_____

8. What are some inspirational themes you would like to see
   treated in future books? _____

_____

_____

9. Would you be interested in reading other **Heartsong
   Presents** titles?   ❏ Yes   ❏ No

10. Please check your age range:
        ❏ Under 18   ❏ 18-24
        ❏ 25-34   ❏ 35-45
        ❏ 46-55   ❏ Over 55

Name _____

Occupation _____

Address _____

City, State, Zip _____

E-mail _____

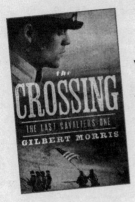

Hearts♥ng

Any 6 Heartsong Presents titles for only $20.95*

GET MORE FOR LESS FROM YOUR HISTORICAL ROMANCE!

Buy any assortment of six *Heartsong Presents* titles and save 25% off the already discounted price of $3.99 each!

*plus $4.00 shipping and handling per order and sales tax where applicable. If outside the U.S. please call 740-922-7280 for shipping charges.

HEARTSONG PRESENTS TITLES AVAILABLE NOW:

(If ordering from this page, please remember to include it with the order form.)

Presents

Great Inspirational Romance
at a Great Price!

Heartsong Presents Heartsong Presents books are inspirational romances in contemporary and historical settings, designed to give you an enjoyable, spirit-lifting reading experience. You can choose wonderfully written titles from some of today's best authors like Wanda E. Brunstetter, Mary Connealy, Susan Page Davis, Cathy Marie Hake, Joyce Livingston, and many others.

When ordering quantities less than six, above titles are $3.99 each.
Not all titles may be available at time of order.

HEARTSONG
PRESENTS

If you love Christian romance...

$12.99

You'll love Heartsong Presents' inspiring and faith-filled romances by today's very best Christian authors...Wanda E. Brunstetter, Mary Connealy, Susan Page Davis, Cathy Marie Hake, and Joyce Livingston, to mention a few!

When you join Heartsong Presents, you'll enjoy four brand-new, mass-market, 176-page books—two contemporary and two historical—that will build you up in your faith when you discover God's role in every relationship you read about!

Mass Market 176 Pages

Imagine...four new romances every four weeks—with men and women like you who long to meet the one God has chosen as the love of their lives...all for the low price of $12.99 postpaid.

To join, simply visit www.heartsong presents.com or complete the coupon below and mail it to the address provided.

YES! Sign me up for Heartsong!

NEW MEMBERSHIPS WILL BE SHIPPED IMMEDIATELY!
Send no money now. We'll bill you only $12.99 postpaid with your first shipment of four books. Or for faster action, call 1-740-922-7280.

NAME _____

ADDRESS _____

CITY _____ STATE _____ ZIP _____

MAIL TO: HEARTSONG PRESENTS, P.O. Box 721, Uhrichsville, Ohio 44683
or sign up at WWW.HEARTSONGPRESENTS.COM